The Adventures of Huckleberry Finn

頑童歷險記

Mark Twain

商務印書館

This Chinese edition of *The Adventures of Huckleberry Finn* has been published with the written permission of Black Cat Publishing.

Name of Book: The Adventures of Huckleberry Finn
Author: Mark Twain
Editors: Victoria Bradshaw
Design and art direction: Nadia Maestri
Computer graphics: Sara Blasigh
Illustrations: Alfredo Belli
Picture research: Sara Blasigh, Laura Lagomarsino
Edition: ©2006 Black Cat Publishing,
an imprint of Cideb Editrice, Genoa, Canterbury

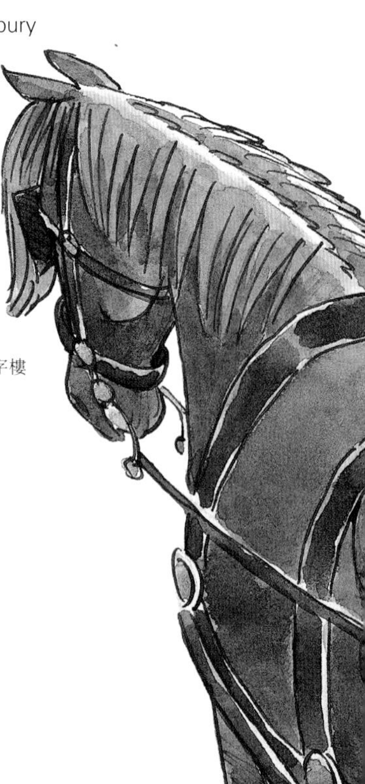

系 列 名：Black Cat 優質英語階梯閱讀 · Level 1
書　　名：頑童歷險記
責任編輯：畢　琦
封面設計：張　毅
出　　版：商務印書館（香港）有限公司
香港筲箕灣耀興道 3 號東滙廣場 8 樓
http://www.commercialpress.com.hk
發　　行：香港聯合書刊物流有限公司
香港新界大埔汀麗路 36 號中華商務印刷大廈 3 字樓
印　　刷：中華商務彩色印刷有限公司
香港新界大埔汀麗路 36 號中華商務印刷大廈
版　　次：2013 年 5 月第 1 版第 2 次印刷

ISBN 978 962 07 1797 0
Printed in Hong Kong

出版説明

本館一向倡導優質閱讀，近年來連續推出了以“Q”為標識的“Quality English Learning 優質英語學習”系列，其中《讀名著學英語》叢書，更是香港書展入選好書，讀者反響令人鼓舞。推動社會閱讀風氣，推動英語經典閱讀，藉閱讀拓廣世界視野，提高英語水平，已經成為一種潮流。

然良好閱讀習慣的養成非一日之功，大多數初中級程度的讀者，常視直接閱讀厚重的原著為畏途。如何給年輕的讀者提供切實的指引和幫助，如何既提供優質的學習素材，又提供名師的教學方法，是當下社會關注的重要問題。 針對這種情況，本館特別延請香港名校名師，根據多年豐富的教學經驗，精選海外適合初中級英語程度讀者的優質經典讀物，有系統地出版了這套叢書，名為《Black Cat 優質英語階梯閱讀》。

《Black Cat 優質英語階梯閱讀》體現了香港名校名師堅持經典學習的教學理念，以及多年行之有效的學習方法。既有經過改寫和縮寫的經典名著，又有富創意的現代作品；既有精心設計的聽、説、讀、寫綜合練習，又有豐富的歷史文化知識；既有彩色插圖、繪圖和照片，又有英美專業演員朗讀作品的 CD。適合口味不同的讀者享受閱讀之樂，欣賞經典之美。

《Black Cat 優質英語階梯閱讀》由淺入深，逐階提升，好像參與一個尋寶遊戲，入門並不難，但要真正尋得寶藏，需要投入，更需要堅持。只有置身其中的人，才能體味純正英語的魅力，領略得到真寶的快樂。當英語閱讀成為自己生活的一部分，英語水平的提高自然水到渠成。

商務印書館（香港）有限公司
編輯部

使用説明

1 應該怎樣選書？

按閱讀興趣選書

《Black Cat優質英語階梯閱讀》精選世界經典作品，也包括富於創意的現代作品；既有膾炙人口的小説、戲劇，又有非小説類的文化知識讀物，品種豐富，內容多樣，適合口味不同的讀者挑選自己感興趣的書，享受閱讀的樂趣。

按英語程度選書

《Black Cat優質英語階梯閱讀》現設Level 1至Level 6，由淺入深，涵蓋初、中級英語程度。讀物分級採用了國際上通用的劃分標準，主要以詞彙（vocabulary）和結構（structures）劃分。

Level 1至Level 3出現的詞彙較淺顯，相對深的核心詞彙均配上中文解釋，節省讀者查找詞典的時間，以專心理解正文內容。在註釋的幫助下，讀者若能流暢地閱讀正文內容，就不用擔心這一本書程度過深。

Level 1至Level 3出現的動詞時態形式和句子結構比較簡單。動詞時態形式以現在時（present simple）、現在時進行式（present continuous）、過去時（past simple）為主，句子結構大部分是簡單句（simple sentences）。此外，還包括比較級和最高級（comparative and superlative forms）、可數和不可數名詞（countable and uncountable nouns）以及冠詞（articles）等語法知識點。

Level 4至Level 6出現的的動詞時態形式，以現在完成時（present perfect）、現在完成時進行式（present perfect continuous）、過去完成時（past perfect continuous）為主，句子結構大部分是複合句（compound sentences）、條件從句（1st and 2nd conditional sentences）等。此外，還包括情態動詞（modal verbs）、被動形式（passive forms）、動名詞

(gerunds)、短語動詞（phrasal verbs）等語法知識點。

根據上述的語法範圍，讀者可按自己實際的英語水平，如詞彙量、語法知識、理解能力、閱讀能力等自主選擇，不再受制於學校年級劃分或學歷高低的約束，完全根據個人需要選擇合適的讀物。

2 怎樣提高閱讀效果？

閱讀的方法主要有兩種：一是泛讀，二是精讀。兩者各有功能，適當地結合使用，相輔相成，有事半功倍之效。

泛讀，指閱讀大量適合自己程度（可稍淺，但不能過深）、不同內容、風格、體裁的讀物，但求明白內容大意，不用花費太多時間鑽研細節，主要作用是多接觸英語，減輕對它的生疏感，鞏固以前所學過的英語，讓腦子在潛意識中吸收詞彙用法、語法結構等。

精讀，指小心認真地閱讀內容精彩、組織有條理、遣詞造句又正確的作品，着重點在於理解"準確"及"深入"，欣賞其精彩獨到之處。精讀時，可充分利用書中精心設計的練習，學習掌握有用的英語詞彙和語法知識。精讀後，可再花十分鐘朗讀其中一小段有趣的文字，邊唸邊細心領會文字的結構和意思。

《Black Cat 優質英語階梯閱讀》中的作品均值得精讀，如時間有限，不妨嘗試每兩個星期泛讀一本，輔以每星期挑選書中一章精彩的文字精讀。要學好英語，持之以恆地泛讀和精讀英文是最有效的方法。

3 本系列的練習與測試有何功能？

《Black Cat 優質英語階梯閱讀》特別注重練習的設計，為讀者考慮周到，切合實用需求，學習功能強。每章後均配有訓練聽、說、讀、寫四項技能的練習，分量、難度恰到好處。

聽力練習分兩類，一是重聽故事回答問題，二是聆聽主角對話、書信朗讀、或模擬記者訪問後寫出答案，旨在以生活化的練習形式逐步提高聽力。每本書均配有 CD 提供作品朗讀，朗讀者都是專業演員，英國作品由英國演員錄音，美國作品由美國演員錄音，務求增加聆聽的真實感和感染力。多聆聽英式和美式英語兩種發音，可讓讀者熟悉二者的差異，逐漸培養分辨英美發音的能力，提高聆聽理解的準確度。此外，模仿錄音朗讀故事或模仿主人翁在戲劇中的對白，都是訓練口語能力的好方法。

閱讀理解練習形式多樣化，有縱橫字謎、配對、填空、字句重組等等，注重訓練讀者的理解、推敲和聯想等多種閱讀技能。

寫作練習尤具新意，教讀者使用網式圖示（spidergrams）記錄重點，採用問答、書信、電報、記者採訪等多樣化形式，鼓勵讀者動手寫作。

書後更設有升級測試（Exit Test）及答案，供讀者檢查學習效果。充分利用書中的練習和測試，可全面提升聽、説、讀、寫四項技能。

4 本系列還能提供甚麼幫助？

《Black Cat 優質英語階梯閱讀》提倡豐富多元的現代閱讀，巧用書中提供的資訊，有助於提升英語理解力，擴闊視野。

每本書都設有專章介紹相關的歷史文化知識，經典名著更有作者生平、社會背景等資訊。書內富有表現力的彩色插圖、繪圖和照片，使閱讀充滿趣味，部分加上如何解讀古典名畫的指導，增長見識。有的書還提供一些與主題相關的網址，比如關於不同國家的節慶源流的網址，讓讀者多利用網上資源增進知識。

Contents

The test is recorded in full. 故事錄音

These symbols indicate the beginning and end of the extracts linked to the listening activities. 聽力練習開始和結束的標記

About the Author

Mark Twain was the pen name of Samuel Langhorne Clemens. He was born on 30 November 1835 in Florida, Missouri, but when he was four years old, he moved with his family to Hannibal, Missouri, a town on the Mississippi River.

In 1861, Mark Twain had to leave Hannibal because of the start of the Civil War. Four years later, the writer had his first literary success when several newspapers published his short story "Jim Smiley and his Jumping Frog." The story was also included in his first book, *The Celebrated Jumping Frog of Calaveras County and other Sketches* (1867).

In 1870 Mark Twain married Olivia Langdon and a year later the couple moved to Hartford, Connecticut, where they lived for the next twenty years. It was during this period that Twain published his best-known works. These include *The Adventures of Tom Sawyer* (1876) and *Life on the Mississippi* (1883). Both of these novels were influenced by the author's childhood experiences in Missouri. Two other historical novels were also published: *The Prince and the Pauper* (1881) and *A Connecticut Yankee in King Arthur's Court* (1889).

Considered by many to be his masterpiece, *Adventures of Huckleberry Finn* (1884) was also published during these years. A sequel [1] to *The Adventures of Tom Sawyer*, this novel is told from the point of view of its protagonist [2], Huckleberry Finn. The character of Huckleberry is based on a boy Twain knew during his childhood in Hannibal. The book is extraordinary for its vivid portrayal [3] of Huck and of life on the river during the author's times.

Loved by both young and old, Mark Twain's novels and short stories reflect the good and the bad in human nature. Filled with humor, but also sadness, his works communicate both the joy and difficulties of human experience.

Mark Twain died on 21 April 1910 in Redding, Connecticut. He was seventy-four years old.

1 Complete Mark Twain's identity card.

Name	0	Samuel Langhorne Clemens
Date and place of birth	1	....
Date and place of death	2	....
Wife's name	3	....
First book published	4	....
Some important works	5	....

1. **sequel**：續集、續篇。
2. **protagonist**：主角。
3. **portrayal**：描述。

The Map

The towns in *italics* are fictional places created by Mark Twain.

The Characters

Huckleberry Finn

Tom Sawyer

Huck's father

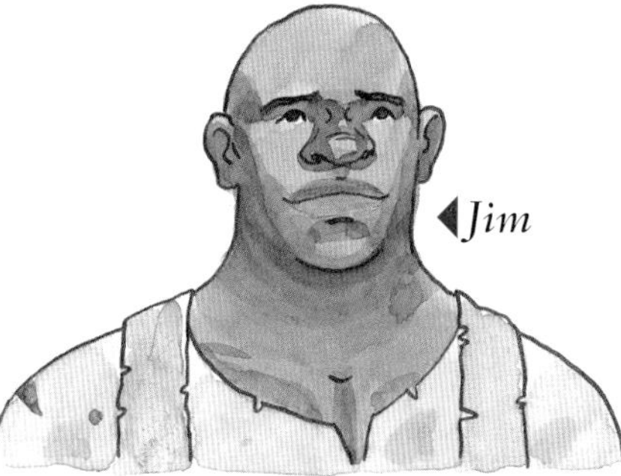
Jim

The king

The duke

BEFORE YOU READ

Match the words in the box to the pictures. Write the words in the spaces next to each picture.

woods cross footprint devil cave

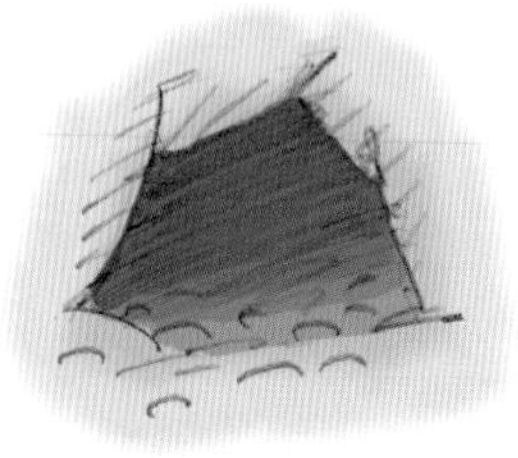

1 ....

2 ....

3 ....

4 ....

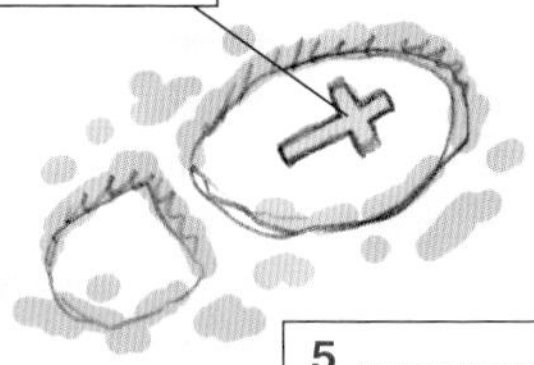

5 ....

Now match the words above to their definitions. Write the number of the picture next to the correct definition.

A ☐ An area of land covered with trees.
B ☐ A religious symbol.
C ☐ A mark made by your foot if you step on a soft surface.
D ☐ An evil spirit some people believe in.
E ☐ A large opening in a rock.

CHAPTER **ONE**

Huck, Tom and Jim

3

My name is Huckleberry Finn and I live in a small town on the Mississippi River called St Petersburg. My friend Tom Sawyer also lives there. We don't get bored often because we have lots of adventures and we like to think of new games to play together. He lives with his Aunt Polly and I live with the Widow [1] Douglas and her sister, Miss Watson. I live with them because my mother is dead and nobody knows where my father is.

It's not easy to live in a house because I like being outside most of the time. Before I came to live with the widow and her sister, I didn't have a house, so nobody told me what to do. Now the two women always tell me what to do. Miss Watson often

1. **Widow**：寡婦。

says, "Huck, do your spelling lessons!" She wants me to do what she says all the time. This is difficult, so sometimes I'm sad. It's also difficult to go to school. But the Widow Douglas thinks school is good for me. I'm learning to spell, read and write a little, and I'm also learning some math.

I'm only a boy, but I have a lot of money. Tom and I found $12,000 in a cave once. It's ours now and we each have $6,000. A man named Judge Thatcher is keeping mine for me because I'm still just a boy.

I know my father wants my money, so it's a good thing he isn't here. Before I found the money, he often hit me. I hid [1] in the woods most of the time when he was here. I'm sorry I can't tell you I never saw him again, because I did. This is the story of all the adventures I had because my father returned.

It all started one winter morning. After breakfast, I went into the garden. There was snow on the ground and I saw a footprint [2]. I looked down and saw the shape of a cross in one of the footprints. It was made to keep the devil away. Suddenly, I was very afraid. I knew

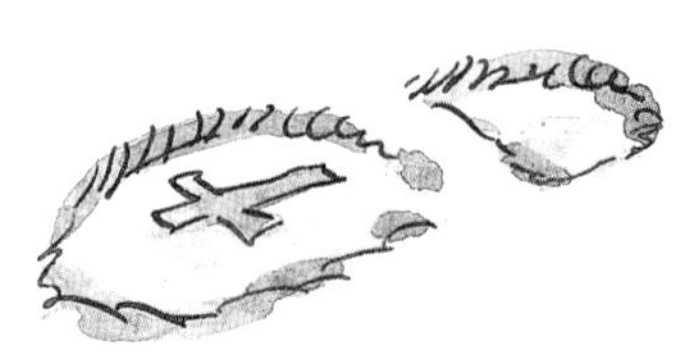

1. **hid**：躲藏。
2. **footprint**：腳印。

that footprint well. It was my father's.

I needed help and there was only one person I could ask. That person was Jim, Miss Watson's slave.[1] Jim was a tall black man. He had a ball made of animal hair. The ball knew everything about the future. I wanted to ask Jim about my future and my father's.

So that night I went to see Jim in his room.

"My father is here again. I know because I found his footprints in the snow," I cried.

Jim listened to his ball and said, "Your old father doesn't know what to do. Sometimes he wants to go away and sometimes he wants to stay."

1. **slave**：奴隸。

"What about me?" I asked.

"The ball says your future will be very difficult, but also very happy. Don't go near the river because there's trouble there," Jim answered.

I went to my room. I felt very afraid again. I opened the door and suddenly saw the man I was so afraid of. He was sitting on my bed. It was my father!

UNDERSTANDING THE TEXT

PET

Decide if each sentence is correct or incorrect. If it is correct, tick (✔) A; if it is incorrect, tick (✔) B. There is an example at the beginning (0).

		A	B
0	Huckleberry Finn lives in a small town near the Pacific Ocean.	☐	✔
1	He is friends with Tom Sawyer.	☐	☐
2	He lives with the Widow Douglas and her sister.	☐	☐
3	Huck's mother and father are both dead.	☐	☐
4	Miss Watson always tells Huck what to do.	☐	☐
5	Huck finds it difficult to go to school.	☐	☐
6	He doesn't think he is learning anything at school.	☐	☐
7	Tom and Huck are both very poor.	☐	☐
8	Huck's father never hits him.	☐	☐
9	Jim is Miss Watson's slave.	☐	☐
10	Jim told Huck his future was happy with no problems.	☐	☐

LISTENING

Huck has to do many things in the house. Listen to the Widow Douglas telling Huck what to do and number the pictures in the correct order.

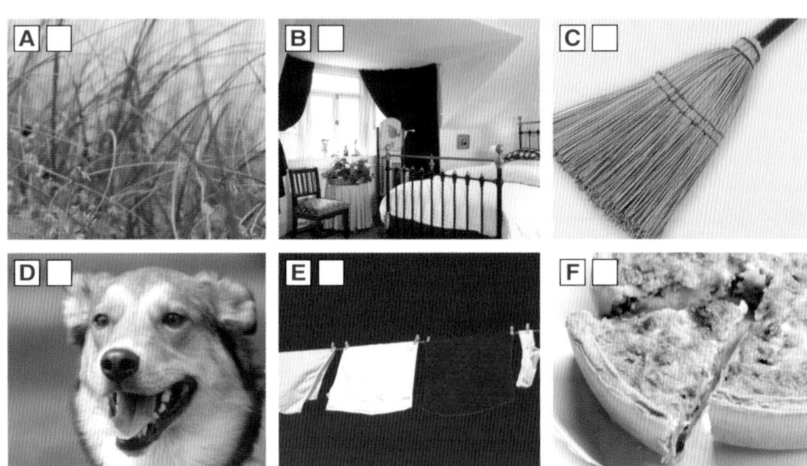

YOU'RE A LOTTERY WINNER!

What would $6,000 be worth today? To find out, multiply it by twenty. ($1 in those days would be worth $20 today.) Write your total in the space provided.

$6,000 x 20 = ...

Imagine you win this amount of money on the lottery. What would you like to spend it on? Below are pictures of some things you could buy with the amount of money you just calculated. Look at each picture and decide which one you like best.

WRITING

Look back at your answer above and write a short letter to Huck. Tell him why you made this choice and not the others. If you prefer, you may write him a letter telling him about some other way in which you would spend your money. Write your letter in about 100 words.

Dear Huck, ...

....

....

Yours,

....

SUMMARY

What happens in Chapter One? Match a sentence in column A to a sentence in column B.

A		B	
1	Huck and Tom	A	wants Huck's money.
2	Huck lives with	B	looking after Huck's money.
3	Huck and Tom have	C	don't get bored very often.
4	Judge Thatcher is	D	told Huck his future.
5	Huck's father	E	saw a footprint in the snow.
6	One morning Huck	F	saw his father.
7	Miss Watson's slave, Jim,	G	a lot of money.
8	Huck went to his room and	H	the Widow Douglas and Miss Watson.

6 LANGUAGE

Unscramble the verbs below to get their infinitive forms.

1 viel ....

2 nlaer ....

3 difn ....

4 tih ....

5 tsrat ....

6 islten ....

7 eihd ....

7

Choose one from the above verbs which best fits each sentence below. Complete each one with either the Present Simple（一般現在式） or Past Simple（一般過去式） forms of your unscrambled verbs. There is an example at the beginning (0).

0 Huck ....lives...... with Miss Watson and the Widow Douglas.

1 Huck .... some money in a cave once.

2 Huck's troubles .... when he saw his father's footprint in the snow.

3 Jim .... to his ball of animal hair before he told Huck his future.

4 Huck's father is a violent man who often .... his son.

5 Huck never .... how to spell until he went to school.

6 Huck often .... in the woods because his father hits him.

BEFORE YOU READ

1 **Match the words in the box to the pictures. Then complete this crossword using the words. All of the words come from Chapter Two. Some letters are already in the crossword to help you.**

saw pig canoe gun ax blood hole beard

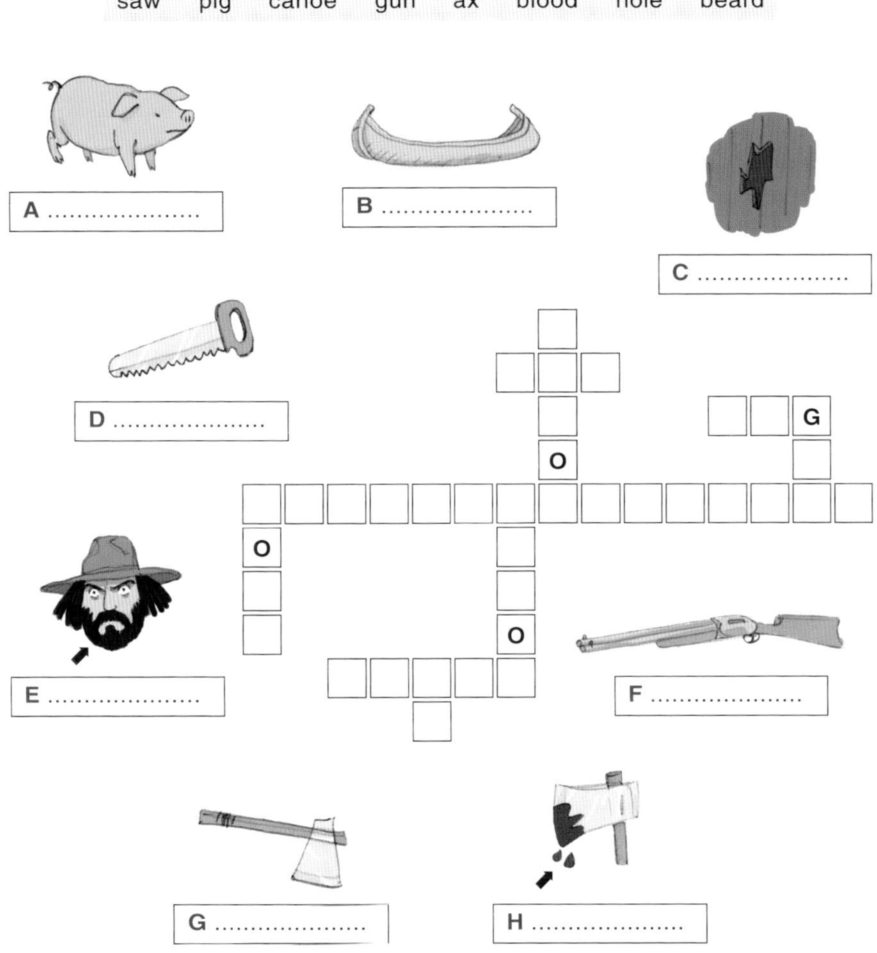

Five across spells the name of one of the characters in this story. Who is it?

CHAPTER **TWO**

A Clever Escape

5

I saw my father so long ago, but I knew he was the man I was looking at now. He was about fifty, and had long, dirty black hair and a black beard. His face was very white and he was wearing very old clothes. His shoes had holes in them and so did his hat. He looked at me, then said, "So, you're wearing clean new clothes."

"Yes, the Widow Douglas bought them for me," I answered.

"I know. I also know she's sending you to school. You must think you're better than your father now," he said.

Without thinking, I answered, "Maybe I do and maybe I don't."

"I'm your father, not that Widow Douglas. You're my son again now and all sons do what their fathers tell them," he said.

I was even more afraid now, so I said, "Yes, father."

I was afraid to look at him. He got up and said, "I know Judge

Thatcher has your money. I'm your father, so it's my money now."

Then he turned and left. I knew he was going to get drunk.[1]

The next morning he went to Judge Thatcher's house. He tried to get my $6,000 but the judge didn't let him have it. I was happy because I knew Judge Thatcher and the Widow Douglas were not afraid of my father.

It was a good thing the judge and the widow also helped to keep me in school. But one day in the spring my father found me on my way to school. He took me up the river in a boat, and then he made me go into the woods with him. We walked for a long time and came to an old, empty cabin[2] made of wood. He made me stay there for many days and nights.

My clean new clothes became old and dirty. I didn't go to school anymore and I started to say bad words again. My father started to hit me more and more often. Once he left me in the house for three days. I finally decided to run away.

My father was always careful not to leave any knives in the house whenever he left me there. But one day I found an old saw. I decided I could make a hole through the wall with it.

The next morning my father told me to go to the river and catch some fish for breakfast. While I was by the river, I suddenly saw an empty canoe on the river. This was my chance. I decided to hide the canoe and use it that night.

Later my father went into town and left me in the house. I got out my saw and started to work on my hole. Soon I climbed out of the cabin through the hole. I didn't leave any footprints because there was grass on the ground all the way to the canoe.

1. **get drunk**：喝醉。
2. **cabin**：小木屋。

I had my father's gun with me. I went into the woods to hunt [1] a pig. I took the pig back to the cabin and let the pig's blood fall on the ground. Then, I pulled some of my hair out and put it on my father's ax with some of the pig's blood.

I took the pig outside and let it fall into the river. I hoped people might think the pig's blood was mine and think I was dead. I waited for night. Then I got in the canoe and went to Jackson's Island.

All that work made me very tired. I got out of the canoe and went into the woods. I found a place on the grass and went to sleep.

1. **hunt**：打獵。

UNDERSTANDING THE TEXT

PET

1 **Choose the best answer (A, B, C or D). There is an example at the beginning (0).**

0 When Huck saw his father, he
- A ☐ didn't know who he was.
- B ☐ thought he looked old.
- C ☑ knew who he was immediately.
- D ☐ decided to run away.

1 Huck's father had
- A ☐ clean new clothes on.
- B ☐ short, blond hair.
- C ☐ holes in his shoes.
- D ☐ short hair and a long beard.

2 Huck's father wanted Huck to
- A ☐ do what he told him to do.
- B ☐ do what the Widow Douglas told him to do.
- C ☐ always live with the Widow Douglas.
- D ☐ be free and happy.

3 Huck's father thought
- A ☐ Huck didn't want his money.
- B ☐ Huck could keep his money.
- C ☐ Huck was poor.
- D ☐ Huck's money was his now.

4 Judge Thatcher
- A ☐ gave Huck's father the money.
- B ☐ didn't let Huck's father have the money.
- C ☐ gave Huck's money to the Widow Douglas.
- D ☐ spent all of Huck's money.

5 On Huck's way to school, his father took him
- A ☐ to the Widow Douglas's house in the woods.
- B ☐ to an empty house in the woods.
- C ☐ hunting in the woods.
- D ☐ to school.

6 Huck made a hole in the wall with

A ☐ a knife.
B ☐ an ax.
C ☐ a saw.
D ☐ a gun.

7 When Huck escaped, he left

A ☐ a lot of footprints on the ground.
B ☐ no footprints because of the grass.
C ☐ no footprints because of the leaves.
D ☐ a lot of footprints in the snow.

8 Huck hunted a pig so he could

A ☐ cook it for dinner for himself and his father.
B ☐ leave it as a present for his father.
C ☐ take it with him to Jackson's Island.
D ☐ make people believe he was dead.

2 SUMMARY

In Chapter Two we find out that Huck thought of a clever way to run away and to make people think he was dead. Read what Huck did (1-6) and match each sentence to why he did it (A-F). Then put the actions in the correct order.

1 He found an empty canoe on the river.
2 He put some of the pig's blood and his own hair on his father's ax.
3 Huck used a saw to make a hole in the wall.
4 He hunted a pig.
5 He threw the pig into the river.
6 Huck waited until it was dark.

A He wanted the people to believe the animal's blood was his.
B He wanted to use this to go to Jackson's Island.
C He didn't want anyone to find the dead animal.
D He did this to get out of the old house his father kept him in.
E He could make people think someone killed him with this object.
F He didn't want anyone to see him leave.

1 ☐☐ 2 ☐☐ 3 ☐☐ 4 ☐☐ 5 ☐☐ 6 ☐☐

OPPOSITES

What are the opposites of the adjectives in the box? Complete the sentences with the opposites of each of the words.

clean alive stupid good old careless full

1 Huck found an .... canoe and he decided to take it.
2 The Widow Douglas was nice to Huck and bought him .... clothes.
3 Huck's father was .... not to leave knives in the house.
4 Huck's clothes became very .... after his father took him away.
5 After living with his father, Huck started saying .... words again.
6 Huck was able to think of a very .... way to escape.
7 Huck hoped people might think he was .... when they saw the pig's blood on the axe.

BEFORE YOU READ

Look at the pictures below. They show the kinds of boats you might see on the Mississippi River. Each boat has a number. Match the number to the correct word from the box for each boat.

houseboat canoe steamboat

1 .... 2 .... 3 ....

Now match the definitions below to one of the pictures above.

A ☐ A boat with a flat bottom that is used as a floating house.
B ☐ A boat with a steam engine often used on rivers.
C ☐ A thin, small wooden boat for one or two people.

CHAPTER **THREE**

A Surprise Arrival

I **woke up and saw the sun** was high up in the sky. That meant it was after eight o'clock in the morning. The light came down through the trees, but it was still quite dark in the woods. I felt happy because I was free of my father.

I was about to go to sleep again, but suddenly I heard a loud, "boom!" I didn't know how far it was, but suddenly I heard it again! I jumped up and looked at the river through the leaves. I saw a lot of smoke on the water and a steamboat full of people.

"They think I'm dead. They're firing cannon balls [1] into the water to make my dead body come up," I thought.

1. **cannon balls**：炮彈。

Soon the steamboat got close to the island. I saw people I knew on the boat: Tom Sawyer, his Aunt Polly, my father and Judge Thatcher. The boat went around Jackson's Island, then up the river and back to the town. I waited until I knew I was OK before I decided to catch some fish for breakfast.

By the end of the day, I started to feel a little sad because nobody was on the island with me. Three days and nights passed in the same way. I fished, looked for fruit, and looked around the island.

Early in the morning on the fourth day, I went into the woods with my gun. I walked on the leaves and, suddenly, my heart jumped! On the ground was a man. He was sleeping and had a blanket [1] over his head. It was almost daylight. I kept my eyes on him. Soon, he woke up and threw the blanket off his head.

Oh, was I happy to see him! It was Jim, Miss Watson's slave.

"Hello, Jim!" I cried, and jumped out from behind the trees.

He jumped up, very afraid. Then he said,

"Oh please, don't hurt me! I never hurt anyone!"

Well, it didn't take me too long to make him understand I wasn't dead. I was so happy to have someone with me. I talked and talked, but Jim didn't say a word. After I told him my story, we sat on the grass together and had breakfast. Now Jim knew what really happened to me, but I didn't know what happened to him.

"So, Jim, why are you here?" I asked.

"I ran away the night after you did. Old Miss Watson was not very nice to me, but I always thought she didn't want to sell me to anyone. But a slave trader [2] came to her house often in the last few days. So I started to worry. I was right to worry because I found

1. **blanket**：毛毯。
2. **slave trader**：奴隸販子。

out that Miss Watson wanted to sell me for $800 to the trader. When I found out, I decided to run away. I swam across the river to this island and stayed here until you found me."

After we told each other our stories, we climbed up a hill on the island. There we found a cave and made it our home. Now that Jim was with me, my days on the island were much better.

One night we saw an old houseboat coming down the river. We got in our canoe and went over to it. When we climbed in through one of the windows we saw a bed, two old chairs, and lots of things on the floor. A man was on the floor. I thought he was sleeping, but Jim said "I know a dead man when I see one." I suddenly felt very afraid.

He went over to the man and put an old blanket on his face.

"I believe he died two or three days ago. Don't come here because it's a very ugly thing to see," Jim said.

I had no wish to see a dead man. I just helped Jim take a few things we might need.

We climbed out of the houseboat again and went back to the island. Later, when I closed my eyes to go to sleep, I thought of the dead man and wished I knew why he was dead.

UNDERSTANDING THE TEXT

Complete the sentences with words from the box. Then put the sentences in the correct order to make a summary of what Huck did in Chapter Three.

body catch cave followed ghost
listened river sleeping steamboat

A ☐ He convinced Jim that he was not a ....
B ☐ He didn't look at the dead .... on the houseboat.
C ☐ He found a man .... in the woods.
D ☐ He heard a loud noise coming from the ....
E ☐ He .... to Jim's story about Miss Watson.
F ☐ He decided to .... some fish for his breakfast.
G ☐ He .... Jim into the houseboat on the river.
H ☐ He realized the people on the .... were looking for him.
I ☐ He found a .... with Jim and made it into a home.

2 **WRITING**

Greetings from Huck! Complete Huck's postcard to Tom Sawyer. Use the correct form of the verbs from the box.

be (x2) find run sleep have
hope tell know want

Dear Tom,

I'm **1**.............. a lot of adventures with Jim. Just a few days after I **2**.............. away, I **3**.............. Jim. At first, I **4**.............. very afraid because I did not **5**.............. who he **6**.............. . He **7**.............. on the ground with a blanket over his head. He **8**.............. me he ran away because Miss Watson **9**.............. to sell him to a slave trader for $800! I want to help Jim run away first, but I **10**.............. to come home soon so I can tell you all about our adventures.

Yours,
Huck

PET

3 **Complete the sentences with the best word (A, B, C or D). There is an example at the beginning (0).**

0 Huck woke up and ..B.... the sun was high up in the sky.
A looked
B saw
C watched
D stared

1 Huck was about to go to sleep again, ... suddenly he heard a loud "boom!"
A because
B so
C but
D if

2 Huck went into the woods and found a man asleep .... the ground.
A at
B over
C in
D on

3 When he saw the man was Jim, Huck jumped out from .... the trees.
A behind
B under
C above
D on

4 Jim ran away because Miss Watson wanted to sell .... for $800.
A his
B him
C her
D he

5 Jim told Huck not to look .... the dead man in the houseboat.
A at
B on
C to
D with

T: GRADE 4

SPEAKING

Topic – weekend/seasonal activities

You can still see steamboats on the Mississippi River today. Many people like to take steamboat tours of the river, especially during the summer. Talk to your friends about a weekend or seasonal activity you enjoy. Use the questions below to help you.

1 What activity did you choose, and why?
2 What equipment, if any, do you need for your activity?
3 How often do you like to do this activity?
4 Do you plan to continue with this activity
Why not?

Slavery in North America in the 1800s

A slave must work very hard for someone for no money. Today there are very few countries in the world where slavery is still allowed, but in the past it was very common in many countries in the world. When we think of slavery, we often think of the slaves in the southern states of the USA during the 1800s.

The colonists who moved to America needed a lot of people to work on their land. Other colonists did not want to do this work, and the owners also did not want to pay people. So slaves, mainly from Africa, were brought to the country.

The slaves traveled on over-crowded [1] ships and many died during the journey. British merchants [2] made a lot of money from selling the slaves to the American colonists. Once the slaves arrived in America, slave traders took them to markets, where they were bought and sold.

The slaves had to work very hard and were often punished. Many slaves died because of the horrible way they were treated. Another very sad thing was that slaves were often separated from their families. Often mothers, fathers and children went to different states.

Because of their terrible lives many slaves tried to run away. A secret

1. **over-crowded**：極擠擁。
2. **merchants**：商人。

Taking African slaves on board a slave ship,
engraving from Cassel's *History of England* (*c.* 1830).

system called the Underground Railroad [1] was established by people who were against slavery. These people, called "Abolitionists," helped runaway slaves by giving them food and places to hide. As a result many slaves escaped to the northern states and Canada.

The differences of opinion about slavery in the North and the South was one of the reasons for the American Civil War, which began in 1861. The war lasted four years and caused many problems even after it ended. The war started because some southern states tried to separate from the Union. At first, President Abraham Lincoln took the northern states into

1. **railroad**：鐵路。這裏指南北戰爭前反對奴隸制並協助黑奴逃往北方或加拿大的組織。

Illustration of General Lewis Armistead at the Battle of Gettysburg.

the war to try to save the Union, but freeing the slaves became important during the war.

In 1863, President Lincoln signed the Emancipation Proclamation [1]. This document stated that all slaves in the southern states were free. Lincoln knew he had to wait until he won the war, but the Proclamation told the South that the end of slavery was near.

The Civil War ended in 1865. The 13th Amendment [2] was passed the same year the war ended. The amendment made slavery illegal [3] throughout the United States. Life slowly got better for African-Americans, but it took a long time. In 1964 The Civil Rights Act became law. This made discrimination [4] based on race, color, religion or national

1. **Emancipation Proclamation :** 解放宣言。
2. **Amendment** : 修正案。
3. **illegal** : 非法。
4. **discrimination :** 歧視。

origin illegal. A lot of people, especially in the South, protested against this new law and there was a lot of violence. During the 1960s, the Civil Rights Movement with some of the important people connected to it, such as Martin Luther King, Jr. and Malcolm X, became very important in improving the rights of all African-Americans.

1 Decide if each sentence is correct or incorrect. If it is correct, tick (✔) A; if it is incorrect, tick (✔) B.

		A	B
1	The American colonists bought slaves to work on their land.	☐	☐
2	Slaves did not often die on the slave ships that took them to America.	☐	☐
3	Most slaves did not come from Africa.	☐	☐
4	Slave traders often helped slaves to run away.	☐	☐
5	The Underground Railroad was a system used to help slaves run away.	☐	☐
6	Abolitionists wanted slavery to continue.	☐	☐
7	The American Civil War lasted from 1861-1865.	☐	☐
8	The Emancipation Proclamation stated that only people in the South could own slaves.	☐	☐

BEFORE YOU READ

PET

1 **Listen to the beginning of Chapter Four and choose the correct picture (A, B or C).**

1 Where did Huck and Jim want to go?

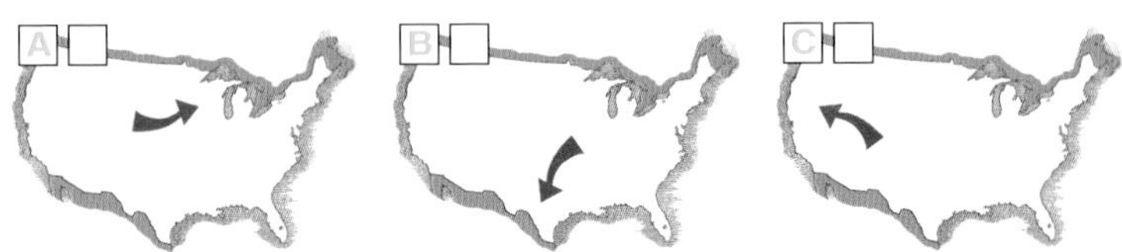

2 What did they want to eat for lunch?

3 Where was Huck when he saw the two men?

4 What was the older man wearing?

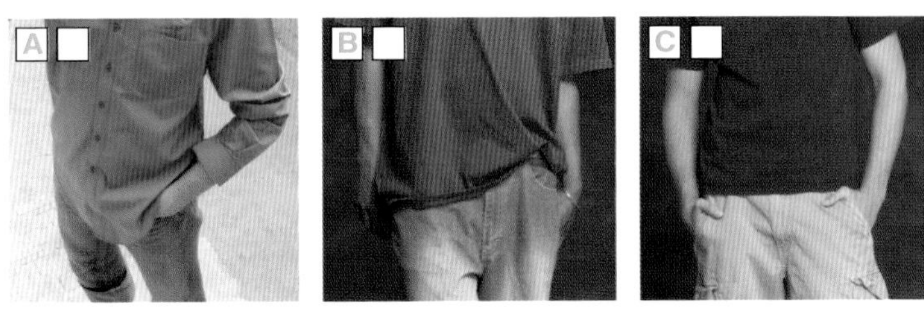

CHAPTER **FOUR**

A Chance Meeting

After I found Jim, the days flew by. [1] We lived just the way we wanted. We left Jackson's Island and went up the river. We wanted to get to the North. [2]

We traveled at night because there were no people on the river then. We did this because Jim was a runaway slave, and we didn't want anyone to see him. During the day we left our canoe somewhere on the river. Then we slept, swam, and later had something to eat.

Early one morning I decided to look for some fruit for lunch. I was in the woods when I saw two men running.

"Quick, please help us. Some men and dogs are running after us, but we didn't do anything," they shouted.

1. **flew by**：過得飛快。
2. **North**：擁有奴隸在北部許多州是非法的。

I had no time to think, so I decided to help them. I felt sorry for the two men. We got back to the camp. Jim made a fire and we sat around it. One of the men was about seventy years old. He was bald[1] and had a gray beard. He had an old hat on, a blue shirt and old blue jeans. The other man was about thirty and was also wearing old clothes. Both of them carried big old bags.

END

By the way the two men looked and talked, we could see they

1. **bald** : 禿頭。

were frauds.[1] But we didn't say anything because we knew they might get us into trouble. I looked at the two men and asked, "What are your names?"

They were quiet for a moment, then the old man said, "Just call me the king and him the duke. You must also be very nice to us because we are a king and a duke."

We knew it wasn't true, but we agreed to call them the

1. **frauds**：騙子。

king and the duke. We made breakfast and tried to do things the way we usually did. The two men asked us a lot of questions. They thought Jim was a runaway slave. I knew these men might get Jim into trouble. People could get a lot of money for a runaway slave. So I decided to tell them Jim was my slave. It was a good thing the two men didn't ask us any more questions. I hoped they believed me, but I wasn't sure.

From the day we met the king and the duke, things got much worse for us. We were often afraid of what the two men might do next. They were bad men and got us into trouble many times. But the worst adventure we had with them was the one I want to tell you about now.

It all started the day the king found out that a rich man from a nearby village named Peter Wilks was dead. The king thought he could find a way to get Wilks's money.

Peter Wilks had three brothers: George, Harvey and William. They were English, but Peter and George moved to America. Before he died, Peter Wilks asked to see his brothers, Harvey and William. William, the youngest brother, was deaf and mute.[1]

But Peter Wilks never saw his two brothers before he died. The funeral[2] was the next day, but Harvey and William were still on their way to America.

The king heard this story and he thought of a way to get Wilks's money. He could pretend to be[3] Harvey and the duke could pretend to be William. So that was how the king, the duke, and I met the Wilks family and got into a lot of trouble.

1. **deaf and mute**：又聾又啞。
2. **funeral**：葬禮。
3. **pretend to be**：假裝。

UNDERSTANDING THE TEXT

1 **Decide if each sentence is correct or incorrect. If it is correct, tick (✔) A; if it is incorrect, tick (✔) B. There is an example at the beginning (0).**

		A	B
0	Huck and Jim thought the men weren't honest.	✔	
1	These two men were members of a royal family.		
2	They were runaway slaves.		
3	They knew Jim was a runaway slave.		
4	The two men wanted to pretend to be Harvey and William Wilks.		
5	Peter Wilks was deaf and mute.		
6	George Wilks also went to America with Peter.		

PET

2 **LANGUAGE**

Complete the conversation using the sentences below (A-F). There is an example at the beginning (0).

Duke: So, how can we get Peter Wilks's money?
King: **0** ....B........
Duke: Don't you think they might not believe us?
King: **1** ....
Duke: But someone might understand that I'm not deaf and mute.
King: **2** ....
Duke: What do you want Huck and Jim to do?
King: **3** ....
Duke: But don't you think Huck might tell everyone we're frauds?
King: **4** ....
Duke: OK, let's do what you say, but I don't want to get caught.
King: **5** ....

A Don't be silly! Just keep your mouth shut and pretend you can't hear.
B By pretending we're Peter's brothers, Harvey and William Wilks.
C They can't know we're frauds because only Peter Wilks knew what his brothers looked like.
D No, he can't say anything because he's afraid for Jim.
E I want them to think the boy is a servant. Jim can hide somewhere.
F That's what you always say.

3 THE KING AND THE DUKE

Read the king's diary entry and complete the spaces with an appropriate word.

10 May 1843

A very good day today. Duke and **1**............. met a teenage boy, called Huck, **2**............. a big black man, Jim. **3**............. the moment I don't really know what they **4**............. doing here, and I don't think they are going to tell **5**............. anything. But I am sure Jim is a runaway slave. I must find out **6**............. much I could get for **7**............. He and the boy are obviously friends and they could both **8**............. very useful, so I don't want **9**............. do anything for the moment. But sooner or later I **10**............. get some money for that slave.

PET

4

Now listen to the duke talking about when he met the king. Choose the best answer (A, B or C).

9

1 When did the duke meet the king?
- A ☐ Last year.
- B ☐ Two or three years ago.
- C ☐ A long time ago.

2 At first, the duke thought the king was
- A ☐ honest.
- B ☐ not interesting.
- C ☐ a fraud.

3 What did the king think of life in the South?
- A ☐ There weren't so many rules as in the North.
- B ☐ The people were very friendly.
- C ☐ He preferred the North.

4 Why was the king looking for someone to travel with him?
- A ☐ Because he was afraid.
- B ☐ Because he didn't like being on his own.
- C ☐ Because he wanted to give the duke some money.

5 Why couldn't the duke find a job?
- A ☐ Because his friends didn't want to help him.
- B ☐ Because he didn't have any experience.
- C ☐ Because he wasn't an honest man.

6 How does the duke justify his life with the king?

A ☐ He doesn't think taking money from others is wrong.
B ☐ He thinks he is very good at his job.
C ☐ He only takes money from rich people.

5 CRIME AND PUNISHMENT

Listen to the four people talking about their crimes. Match each person to one of the crimes in the box.

stealing an apple   killing his wife
stealing a lot of money   helping two slaves to escape

1

....

2

....

3
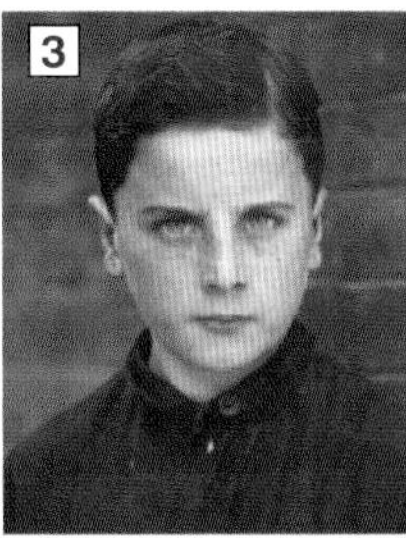
....

4

....

6 Now listen again and answer these questions.

Who:

A ☐ committed his/her crime because of problems in society?
B ☐ committed crimes in different towns?
C ☐ didn't want to commit his/her crime because of love for another person?
D ☐ needed to commit a crime because he/she was hungry?

BEFORE YOU READ

Do you know the words below? All of them appear in Chapter Five. Match the words from the box to the pictures.

coffin   tears   to smile   servant   to hug   to count

1	2	3 ....
4	5	6 ....

Now complete the sentences with one of the words above. Remember to use the correct tense of any verbs.

1 The King told everyone that Huck was his ....
2 Peter Wilks was put inside a .... because he was dead.
3 When Mary Jane saw the king and the duke, she .... them because she thought they were her uncles.
4 .... fell down the king's face when he saw the coffin.
5 The king .... the money in front of everyone.
6 When she gave the king back the money, Mary Jane .... because she was happy.

CHAPTER **FIVE**

The Wilks Family

The morning the king learned about Peter Wilks, he made the duke and me get on a steamboat with him. We left Jim a few miles [1] up the river. He was supposed to wait for a few days until our return.

We got to the village where Peter Wilks died the night before. We got off the steamboat and some men came to meet us. It was clear they knew someone was coming. The king made them think he was Harvey and the duke was William. He also made them believe I was their servant. They all believed him because he spoke like an Englishman and we all wore new clothes.

1. **miles**：英哩。**1**英哩＝**1.609**公里。

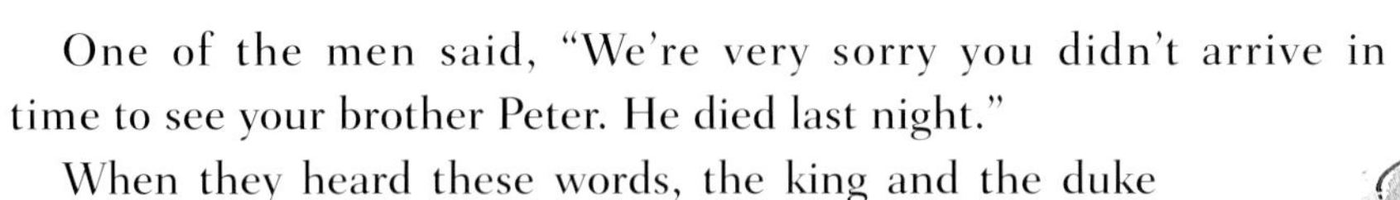

One of the men said, "We're very sorry you didn't arrive in time to see your brother Peter. He died last night."

When they heard these words, the king and the duke started to cry. This made everyone else cry. Then the men took us to the Wilks's house. Three girls stood at the door. The oldest said, "We're Uncle George's daughters. Our father and mother died last year so we live here now."

The king already knew all about them, so he said, "Oh, you must be Mary Jane."

"Yes, and these are my sisters: Susan and Joanna," answered Mary Jane.

The three girls hugged the king and the duke. All of them cried together and so did the townspeople. Then the king lifted his head and saw Uncle Peter's coffin in the corner of the room. He took the duke's arm and they slowly walked over to the coffin. They both had tears in their eyes.

I felt bad to see how the king and duke made everyone believe they were Harvey and William. But I also thought how dangerous it might be for me to tell everyone everything.

The king stood up and said, "Thank you all for coming here. We want all of Peter's good friends and family to have dinner with us this evening."

Mary Jane gave the king a letter and said, "Uncle Peter wrote this before he died. He wanted you to have it."

Still with tears in his eyes, the king took the letter and read it in front of everyone.

Then he said, "Oh, my brother was such a good man. You all heard he left $6,000 for William and me. You also heard that he hid the money in the basement."

Nobody said anything. Then the king said, "Uncle William and I must go down to the basement and get the money. We want everything to be out in the open."

So the king, the duke and I went downstairs to the basement. We found the $6,000 in a bag. The king said, "I have a good idea! Let's go back upstairs and give this money to the girls in front of everyone!"

"Yes, then we are sure to make them think we're Harvey and William," answered the duke.

"We can find a way to get the money back later," added the duke.

So we all went upstairs again and the king counted the money in front of everyone and gave it to the girls. This made everyone cry again. Mary Jane was quiet, then she walked up to the king and said,

"Uncle Harvey, I want you to take this money back and spend it in any way you like."

She smiled and gave the king the bag of money.

UNDERSTANDING THE TEXT

Answer these questions.

1 Who did the king, the duke and Huck pretend to be?
2 Why did the men believe the king so easily?
3 What was the relationship between Peter Wilks and the girls in the house?
4 Why did Huck decide not to tell the Wilks family the truth?
5 Where did Peter Wilks leave the money?
6 Why did the king decide to give the money to Mary Jane?
7 What did Mary Jane do with the money?

PET

Read the sentences below and choose the correct word (A, B, C or D) for each space. There is an example at the beginning (0).

0 The king made Huck get on a steamboat ...B... him.
A to
B with
C at
D and

1 Everyone believed the king was Harvey .... he spoke like a person from England.
A although
B but
C because
D even

2 Huck didn't say anything because he thought it .... be dangerous.
A was
B ought
C might
D must

3 Peter Wilks wrote a letter .... he died.
A after
B when
C but
D before

4 The king counted the money in front of ....
A someone
B nobody
C anyone
D everyone

5 The king had a good ....
A thought
B decision
C idea
D answer

CHARACTERS

Complete the sentences with the name of the character who did the action described.

A .... introduced her sisters, Susan and Joanna, to the king, the duke and Huck.

B The .... made .... and the .... get on a steamboat with him.

C .... gave the king the letter Peter Wilks wrote before he died.

D .... felt bad because everyone believed the king and the duke were Peter Wilks's brothers.

E The .... wanted to give George Wilks's daughters the $6,000.

F The .... made the men believe that he was Harvey and the .... was William.

G The .... and the .... cried when they heard Peter Wilks was dead.

H .... gave the king back the $6,000.

Now put the above sentences in the order in which they happened in the chapter.

1 [B] 2 [ ] 3 [ ] 4 [ ] 5 [ ] 6 [ ] 7 [ ] 8 [ ]

4 LANGUAGE

Look at the rules for using some and any. Then complete the sentences below.

SOME	**ANY**
(somebody, something, somewhere)	(anybody, anything, anywhere)
– generally used in **affirmative** phrases	– generally used in **questions** and negative phrases with **not**
I found ***some*** *biscuits in the cupboard*	*Are there* ***any*** *biscuits in the cupboard?* *I did not find* ***any*** *biscuits in the cupboard.*

A I did not want .... to open the door.

B .... just rang the doorbell.

C I'd open the door, but I know my keys are .... inside.

D I did not want .... doorbells to ring while I was sleeping.

E I lost my keys so .... must help me get inside.

BEFORE YOU READ

All of the words below appear in Chapter Six. Match the words in box to their pictures.

auction   graveyard   lightning   tattoo   arrow   mattress

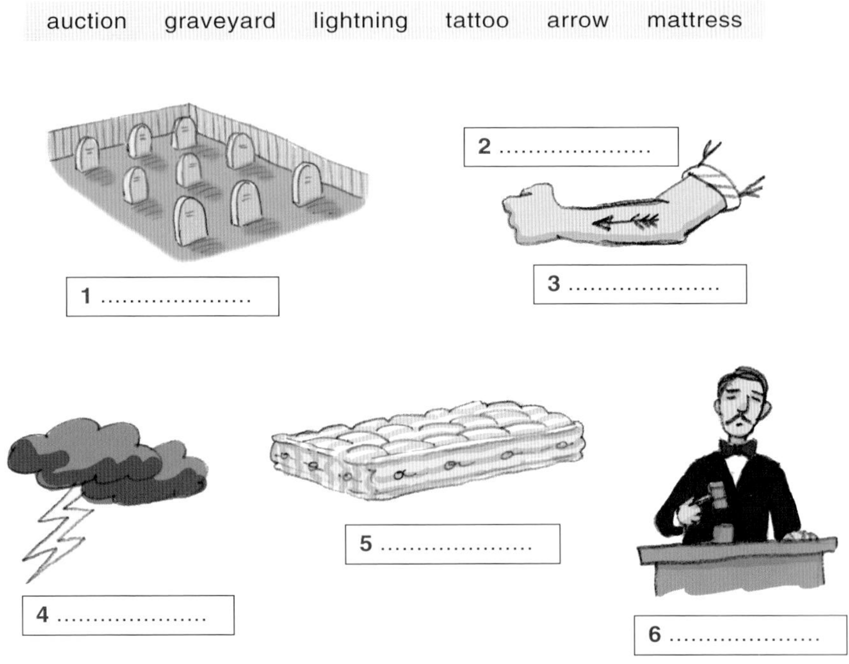

Now write sentences using each of the words above. There is an example at the beginning.

A The lightning in the sky meant that it would rain soon.

B ....

C ....

D ....

E ....

F ....

CHAPTER **SIX**

A Surprise in a Coffin!

12

That night we all had dinner with Peter Wilks's good friends. After dinner, I quietly went upstairs to the king's room. I knew the bag of money was in there somewhere. I felt bad that the king and the duke wanted to steal the money Peter Wilks left for his family. I also felt bad that Mary Jane immediately [1] gave the $6,000 back to the king. So I decided to take the money and hide it.

I thought, "After I leave, I can write to Mary Jane and let her know where I hid the money. That way her family can get it back."

I sat on the king's bed and saw a hole in the mattress [2]. I put my hand inside and felt the bag of money. I took it out and returned to my room. I waited until everyone went to bed. Then I very quietly went downstairs to find a place to hide the money. The

1. **immediately**：立刻。　　2. **mattress**：牀墊。

front door was locked [1] so I had to find another way out. Suddenly, I heard someone on the stairs.

I ran to the living room and saw the coffin in the center of the room. It was slightly open and you could see the dead man's face. I didn't have time to think of where to hide the money, so I put it in the coffin. Then I closed it and hid behind the door. Mary Jane came into the room and sat next to her uncle's coffin. She started to cry softly. I felt very sorry for her. I quickly left the room and went up to bed.

The next day, the funeral took place with no problems. Nobody found the money and the king didn't know it wasn't in his room. On the second day after the funeral, the king held an auction. [2] He wanted to sell Peter's land and hoped to make a lot of money. The auction took place in the afternoon in the town square.

The auction was almost over when a group of men

1. **locked**：鎖住。
2. **auction**：拍賣。

arrived. They brought two men with them, an old one and a young one. One of the men in the group said, "Here are Harvey and William Wilks!"

"These two men are surely frauds!" answered the king.

To me it was clear these two were the real brothers. But what a show the king and duke put on! They made almost everyone believe the two men were frauds. But suddenly the old man said to the king, "If you're Harvey Wilks, tell me, what tattoo did Peter have on his body?"

For the first time, both the king and the duke looked afraid. But the king didn't give up. He smiled and said, "The tattoo is an arrow."

"You're lying!" [1] shouted the old man. Then someone said,

"Wait! There's only one way to discover the truth. We must dig up the coffin to see what's on Peter's body."

Everyone shouted, "Hooray! Let's go!"

So they took the five of us to the graveyard. I was very afraid. I thought, "It's getting dark. This is a good time to try to run away."

But a very big man held my arm. There was no way for me to run away. Some of the men started to dig. It started to rain very heavily but they did not stop.

The men dug up the coffin and opened it. Nobody could see anything because of the rain and the dark. Suddenly lightning lit up the sky. It was just enough time to see the bag of money sitting on the dead man's body. Shouts filled the air! The man suddenly let go of my arm. I started to run very fast.

1. **lying**：撒謊。

It was very dark, but the lightning helped me to see which way to go. The minute I was far enough from the town, I looked for an empty boat and jumped in. Soon I got to the place on the river where Jim was hiding. I jumped in our canoe and shouted, "Quick, Jim. Thank God we're free of them, at last!"

Jim had a big smile on his face. He was so happy to see me again! But we had no time. Just when I thought we were out of danger, the lightning lit up the sky again to show us the king and duke. They climbed into the canoe. Now we knew more trouble was ahead.

UNDERSTANDING THE TEXT

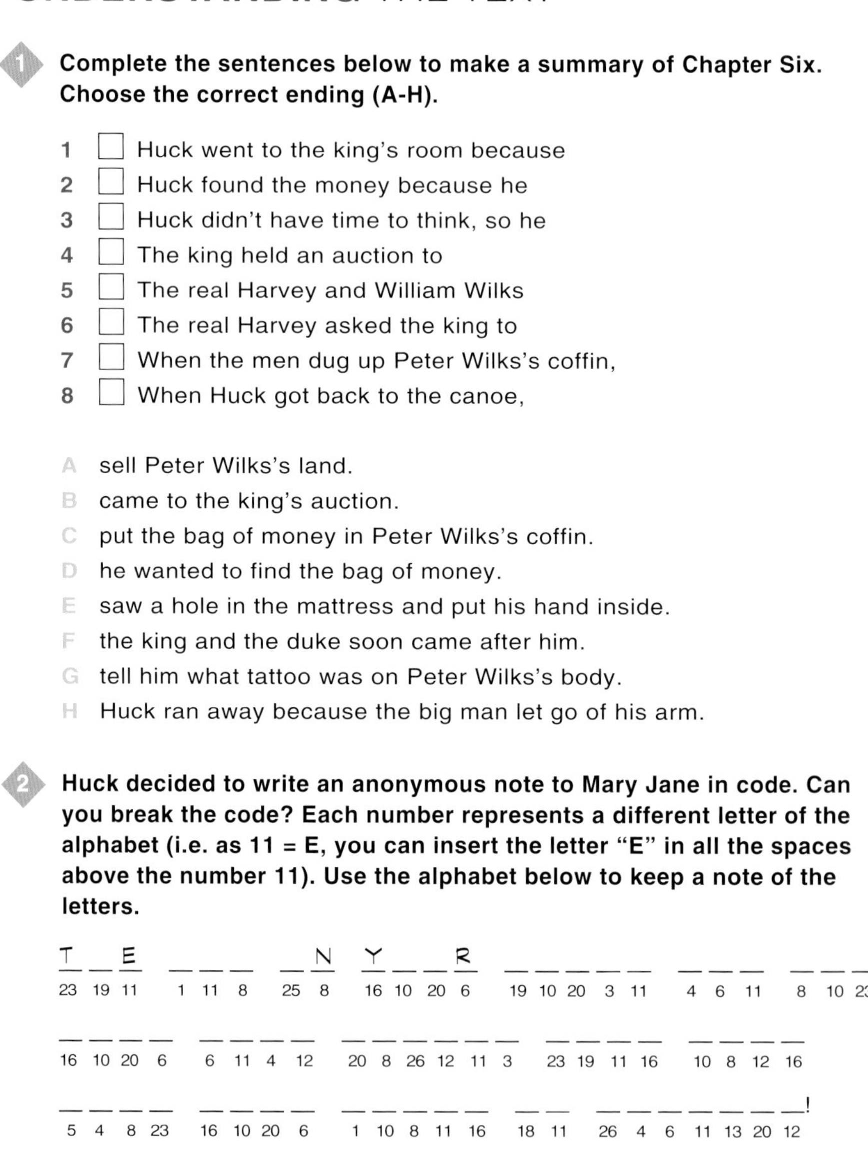

1 Complete the sentences below to make a summary of Chapter Six. Choose the correct ending (A-H).

1 ☐ Huck went to the king's room because
2 ☐ Huck found the money because he
3 ☐ Huck didn't have time to think, so he
4 ☐ The king held an auction to
5 ☐ The real Harvey and William Wilks
6 ☐ The real Harvey asked the king to
7 ☐ When the men dug up Peter Wilks's coffin,
8 ☐ When Huck got back to the canoe,

A sell Peter Wilks's land.
B came to the king's auction.
C put the bag of money in Peter Wilks's coffin.
D he wanted to find the bag of money.
E saw a hole in the mattress and put his hand inside.
F the king and the duke soon came after him.
G tell him what tattoo was on Peter Wilks's body.
H Huck ran away because the big man let go of his arm.

2 Huck decided to write an anonymous note to Mary Jane in code. Can you break the code? Each number represents a different letter of the alphabet (i.e. as 11 = E, you can insert the letter "E" in all the spaces above the number 11). Use the alphabet below to keep a note of the letters.

T _ E   _ _ _   _ N   Y _ _ R   _ _ _ _ _   _ _ _   _ _ _
23 19 11   1 11 8   25 8   16 10 20 6   19 10 20 3 11   4 6 11   8 10 23

_ _ _ _   _ _ _ _   _ _ _ _ _ _   _ _ _ _   _ _ _ _
16 10 20 6   6 11 4 12   20 8 26 12 11 3   23 19 11 16   10 8 12 16

_ _ _ _   _ _ _ _   _ _ _ _ _   _ _   _ _ _ _ _ _ _!
5 4 8 23   16 10 20 6   1 10 8 11 16   18 11   26 4 6 11 13 20 12

A	B	C	D	E	F	G	H	I	J	K	L	M	N	O	P	Q	R	S	T	U	V	W	X	Y	Z
–	–	–	–	11	–	–	–	–	–	–	–	–	8	–	–	–	6	–	23	–	–	–	–	16	–

BEFORE YOU READ

Match the words in the box to the pictures below.

cotton plantation   fence   wagon   tar and feather

1 ....

2 ....

3 ....

4 ....

2 **Now match the words from the exercise above to their descriptions below.**

A ☐ A farm with a large piece of land on which to grow cotton.

B ☐ A wooden structure built around a garden or piece of land.

C ☐ A wooden cart with wheels that is pulled by a train, or, if small, by horses.

D ☐ To cover someone with a black, sticky substance and chicken feathers as a form of punishment.

CHAPTER **SEVEN**

Trouble for Jim

13

After the king and the duke returned, the king was very angry with the duke. He thought the duke stole the bag of money and put it in the coffin. The duke thought the same thing about the king. I was happy because that meant they didn't think I did it.

After their return, life got quite difficult for the king and the duke. They couldn't make any money in their usual, dishonest ways. Things got worse and worse for them. Jim and I became worried because the two of them often whispered [1] to each other. They didn't want us to hear what they said to each other. I didn't say anything to Jim, but I was sure they wanted to sell Jim back

1. **whispered**：低聲說。

into slavery. They knew people could get a lot of money for a runaway slave.

I soon found out I was right. One morning I came back to our camp and saw that Jim was gone. I knew the king and the duke were in a nearby town. They went there to make some money.

I felt so sorry that Jim was gone. I decided to go to the village to try to find out where Jim was. On my way to the village, I saw a boy on the road.

I stopped and asked him, "Did you see a black man around here?"

"Yes, he's a runaway slave and they took him to Phelps Farm, about two miles from here," answered the boy.

"Who gave him up?" I asked.

"An old man. He got $40 for him," answered the boy.

I decided to go straight to Phelps Farm. I didn't know how I could free Jim again, but I knew I had to try. I got to the farm and looked around. It was a sunny, hot day. The farm was a cotton plantation [1] with a white wooden fence around it. I climbed over the fence and walked to the house. I didn't know what to say, but I would think of something.

Suddenly, a woman came out of the house. I thought, "She must be Mrs Phelps and she's running right over here. Oh no, what can I do?"

But I didn't have time to think of anything because she ran right to me and gave me a big hug.

"Oh, you're here at last!" said the woman. Then she added, "Let me look at you, dear nephew."

I didn't know what to say, so I just stood there.

1. **plantation**：大種植園。

"Oh, don't be so shy, Tom! It's not at all like the Sawyers to be shy!" she said, laughing.

I couldn't believe my ears! So the Phelps family expected Tom Sawyer to arrive! How could it be? Now I really didn't know what to do, so I just smiled and said, "Yes, it's really me, Mrs Phelps."

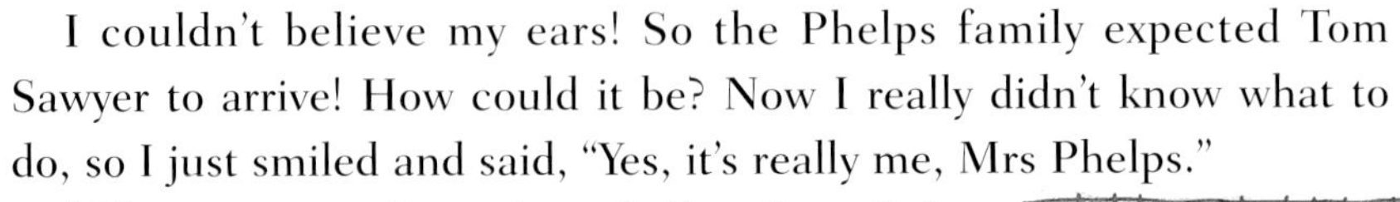

"Oh, you can call me Aunt Sally; after all, I am your aunt," she said.

We went into the house together and I met Uncle Silas. I was so happy they thought I was

Tom Sawyer. It wasn't difficult for me to pretend to be Tom because I knew all about him. I told them all about Tom's Aunt Polly and his brother, Sid. Aunt Sally and Uncle Silas both believed I was Tom.

Suddenly, I heard a steamboat on the river. I thought, "Oh no! Maybe Tom is on that steamboat now and he's coming here! I must make up [1] an excuse to leave so I can tell him what happened."

I looked at Aunt Sally and said, "I have to go back into town to get my suitcase. It was too heavy to carry all the way here."

"Your Uncle Silas can take you on our wagon," said Aunt Sally.

"Thanks, but I know how to drive the horses," I answered.

So I got on the wagon and started for the town. Halfway there I saw Tom Sawyer on the road. His mouth fell open when he saw me.

"You must be a ghost because you're supposed to be dead!" he cried.

1. **make up**：想出。

"No, you can see that I'm not dead," I answered.

"Then what are you doing here?" asked Tom.

"There's not much time to explain. Just get on the wagon and let's go to your Aunt Sally's house. I'll tell you everything on our way there," I answered.

So Tom got on the wagon with me. I started to tell him all about my adventures. But suddenly we saw lots of people down the road. They walked past us and we saw something horrible. They had tarred and feathered the king and the duke! I knew those two were very bad men, but I still felt sorry for them.

UNDERSTANDING THE TEXT

PET

1 **Choose the correct answer (A, B, C or D) for each of the sentences below. There is an example at the beginning (0).**

0 After their return, the king and the duke
- A ☑ each thought the other stole the bag of money.
- B ☐ thought Huck stole the bag of money.
- C ☐ thought Jim stole the bag of money.
- D ☐ thought nobody stole the bag of money.

1 The king and the duke
- A ☐ often whispered to each other.
- B ☐ wanted Jim to become their slave.
- C ☐ sold Jim to the boy Huck met on the road.
- D ☐ were horrible to Jim.

2 The boy Huck met on the road told him
- A ☐ that he gave an old man $40 for Jim.
- B ☐ to go to the village to find Jim.
- C ☐ that Jim was at the Phelps Farm.
- D ☐ that Jim ran away.

3 Huck thought of
- A ☐ something to say as soon as he saw Mrs Phelps.
- B ☐ nothing to say when he saw Mrs Phelps.
- C ☐ telling Mrs Phelps that he was Tom Sawyer.
- D ☐ telling Mrs Phelps that he was Tom's friend.

4 Mrs Phelps thought Huck was
- A ☐ Tom Sawyer's brother, Sid.
- B ☐ Tom Sawyer's friend.
- C ☐ Tom Sawyer.
- D ☐ Tom Sawyer's cousin.

5 She told Huck
- A ☐ to ride a horse back into town to get his suitcase.
- B ☐ to walk back into town with Uncle Silas to get his suitcase.
- C ☐ he could go into town with Uncle Silas on their wagon.
- D ☐ to ride a bicycle into town.

6 On their way back to the Phelps Farm, Huck and Tom saw

A ☐ that the king was tarred and feathered.

B ☐ that both the king and the duke were tarred and feathered.

C ☐ that some people wanted to tar and feather the king and the duke.

D ☐ that the king and the duke were tarred but not feathered.

T: GRADE 4

2 SPEAKING

Topic - work

In Chapter Seven we discover that Phelps Farm is a cotton plantation. Many people worked as farmers in Mark Twain's times. What kind of work do you think is interesting? Talk about it using the questions below to help you.

1 What do you like about this job?

2 Is it an easy or difficult job?

3 Do people who have this job travel a lot?

4 Would you like to have this job? Why? Why not?

PET

3 LANGUAGE

Look at the text on each notice. What does it say? Choose the best answer (A, B or C).

1

Auctions held first Saturday of every month (except January)

A ☐ On any Saturday you can buy something at this auction.

B ☐ You can buy something at this auction only on the first Saturday in January.

C ☐ You can buy something at this auction on the first Saturday of any month, but not in January.

2

Tom,
The canoeing lessons might be cancelled if there aren't enough students. Tell your friends to sign up right away!
Huck

A ☐ Tom can't get into Huck's canoeing class, but his friends might.

B ☐ Tom and his friends should sign up immediately or the canoeing class might be cancelled.

C ☐ If Tom's friends sign up for the canoeing class, it might be cancelled.

3 

A ☐ Boats must proceed with caution beyond this point.

B ☐ All boats must not go any further because of a nearby waterfall.

C ☐ If you want to see the waterfall, you must go beyond this point.

4 

A ☐ Between 7.30 a.m. and 8.30 a.m. on Saturdays three pounds of peas are very cheap.

B ☐ Between 7.30 a.m. and 8.30 a.m. on Saturdays you can buy two pounds of peas for the price of three.

C ☐ Before 7.30 a.m. on Saturdays you can buy peas cheaply.

BEFORE YOU READ

1  **Listen to the beginning of Chapter Eight and complete the spaces with the words you hear.**

By the time we got back to Aunt Sally's house, Tom knew everything. We decided to tell Aunt Sally that Tom was his brother Sid. I took his suitcase and **1**............. it was mine.

Aunt Sally was very surprised to see us both arrive! But she was so happy to have, she thought, both of her **2**............. with her. She put us in the same room together.

That night we went to bed early and waited until everyone **3**............. went to bed. Then we **4**............. out of the window. We looked around, but we didn't know where Jim was. Then Tom cried, "I know where they put Jim! In that shed **5**............. there!"

So we went to the shed and looked inside through a small window. Sure enough, there was Jim. When he saw us, he couldn't **6**............. his eyes!

"It's Huck, and there's Tom too," he cried happily.

"Jim, don't worry. We know how to help you run away," I said.

We **7**............. how we could help him, and then we went back to the house. Every night, we climbed out of our window after everyone went to sleep. We dug a **8**............. into Jim's shed so he could use it to run away.

CHAPTER **EIGHT**

The Great Escape

14

By the time we got back to Aunt Sally's house, Tom knew everything. We decided to tell Aunt Sally that Tom was his brother Sid. I took his suitcase and pretended it was mine.

Aunt Sally was very surprised to see us both arrive! But she was so happy to have, she thought, both of her nephews with her. She put us in the same room together.

That night we went to bed early and waited until everyone else went to bed. Then we climbed out of the window. We looked around, but we didn't know where Jim was. Then Tom cried, "I know where they put Jim! He's in that shed [1] over there!"

So we went to the shed and looked inside through a small

1. **shed**: 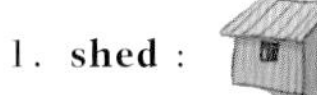 小屋。

window. Sure enough, there was Jim. When he saw us, he couldn't believe his eyes!

"It's Huck, and there's Tom, too," he cried happily.

"Jim, don't worry. We know how to help you run away," I said.

We explained how we could help him, and then we went back to the house. Every night, we climbed out of our window after everyone went to sleep. We dug a hole into Jim's shed so he could use it to run away. END

On the night we wanted to run away, we climbed out the window after everyone went to bed as usual. While we were standing in the garden behind a tree we saw some men with guns.

We knew we had to be very careful. We got to the shed and Jim climbed out of the hole.

As we climbed over the fence the men began to shoot at us and ran after us. We ran to the river, got in our canoe and could still hear the men's shouts. I smiled and hugged [1] Jim.

"Now you're a free man again, Jim," I said.

We were all very happy and Tom cried, "Wow! I even got a bullet [2] in my leg!"

Jim and I were suddenly very worried. I took some old clothes and made a bandage [3] for Tom's leg. He cried, "No! Hurry up, there's no time!"

But Jim didn't want to go. He wanted to find a doctor for Tom first. Tom didn't want us to do it, but finally I agreed with Jim. I took the canoe and went to find a doctor while Jim stayed behind with Tom.

I went back into town and found a doctor. I took him to our canoe, but he saw it and said, "This canoe is too small for two people. Tell me where your friend is. I can go and you can stay here until I return."

I agreed, but I didn't like it. I was so tired I went to sleep behind a tree. When I woke up, I saw the sun in the sky. I slept all night and

1. **hugged**：擁抱。
2. **bullet**：子彈。
3. **bandage**：繃帶。

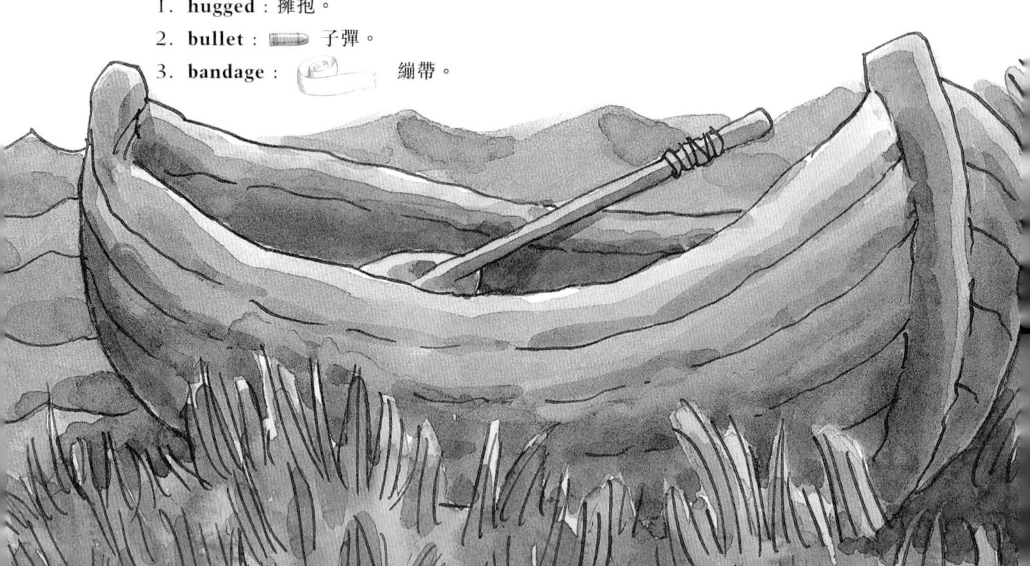

now I didn't know where the doctor was! I decided to go back to Phelps Farm and tell them everything. I thought it was the best way to help Tom.

I got to the farm and saw a lot of people in the garden. Tom, Jim and the doctor were there! The people wanted to hurt Jim. But the doctor stopped them and said, "He may be a runaway slave, but he's a good man. He helped me with the boy's leg."

"Let's lock him in the shed so he can't run away again," said Uncle Silas.

Tom suddenly cried, "You've no right to! Nobody can lock Jim up again because he's not a slave anymore! He was Miss Watson's slave and she died two months ago! Before she died, she made him a free man."

I couldn't believe my ears! And Jim was so happy to know he was a free man! Tom told everyone everything we did and who we were. Now everyone knew everything and we were all very happy. But there was one more thing I was still worried about. I looked at Jim and said, "What do I do now? I can't go back home because of my father. I'm sure he's got my $6,000 from Judge Thatcher."

"Don't you worry, Huck. Your father can't hurt you anymore," said Jim.

"How do you know?" I asked.

"Remember that old houseboat we saw on the river one night? There was a dead man on the floor and I didn't let you look at his face. I didn't let you because it was your father, Huck," said Jim.

And so that was how our adventures came to an end. And we all got our freedom, at last.

UNDERSTANDING THE TEXT

1 SUMMARY

Unscramble the sentences below to make a summary of Chapter Eight. There is an example at the beginning (0).

0 Huck Tom Aunt Sally and believe made were they nephews her
Huck and Tom made Aunt Sally believe they were her nephews.

1 the Jim and Tom shed Huck in found
....

2 Huck the dug a Tom and hole into shed
....

3 When ran they Tom away leg hurt his
....

4 doctor Tom a helped
....

5 found Jim he man was free a out
....

6 found Huck out father was dead his
....

7 freedom everyone their got
....

2 CHARACTERS

Match the characters in the box below to what they said. Some characters are used more than once.

Tom Jim Huck
Uncle Silas the doctor

1 "I know where they put Jim!" ....
2 "Wow! I even got a bullet in my leg!" ....
3 "I can't go back home because of my father." ....
4 "Your father can't hurt you anymore." ....
5 "Let's lock him in the shed so he can't run away again!" ....
6 "He may be a runaway slave, but he's a good man." ....
7 "Nobody can lock Jim up again because he's not a slave anymore." ....
8 "This canoe is too small for two people." ....

PET

Choose the correct word (A, B, C or D) for each space. There is an example at the beginning (0).

0 Tom was proud ..B... he got a bullet in his leg.
- A if
- B that
- C who
- D what

1 Jim and Huck were very ...... about Tom's leg.
- A worried
- B afraid
- C bad
- D surprised

2 Jim wanted to ...... a doctor for Tom.
- A search
- B ask
- C find
- D look

3 The doctor thought the canoe was too ...... for two people.
- A large
- B heavy
- C cheap
- D small

4 Huck was so tired he fell asleep ...... a tree.
- A above
- B close
- C next
- D behind

5 The doctor told ...... that Jim helped him save Tom.
- A all people
- B anyone
- C everyone
- D none

6 Jim was very happy to ...... he was not a slave anymore.
- A new
- B knew
- C knowing
- D know

7 Jim told Huck not to worry ...... his father.
- A of
- B to
- C about
- D for

WRITING

Write a short book report about this book. Include the following information:

- a brief summary of the story;
- what in particular you liked or did not like about the book;
- who your favorite character was and why;
- what kind of person would like this book.

CROSSWORD

Complete this crossword. Look at the clues and pictures. Write the words in the correct place. You do not have any numbers, but use the letters already in the crossword to help you.

1 Jim was not a ...... any more.
2 Huck and Tom ...... a hole in the ground.
3 Both Huck and Jim had their ...... now.
4 Uncle Silas used a key to ...... the door.

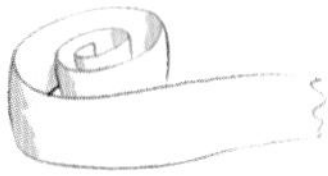

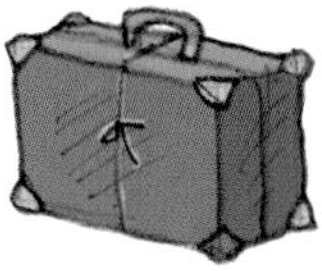

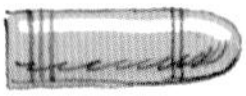

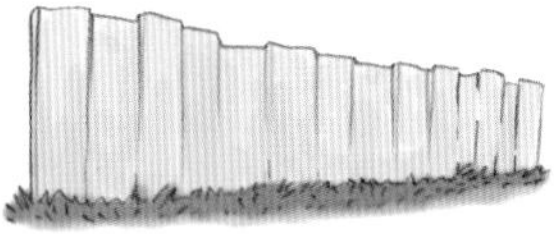

EXIT TEST 1

WHO'S WHO?

Look at the names in the box. Find and circle them in the word square below.

Widow Douglas	Tom	Jim	Huck	Miss Watson
Judge Thatcher	King	Duke	Aunt Sally	

J	D	W	I	D	O	W	D	O	U	G	L	A	S
Y	Y	R	F	Q	V	A	J	L	P	I	J	R	M
L	N	F	J	M	O	T	E	W	X	A	E	J	L
L	W	L	L	V	B	M	H	T	Y	H	D	E	W
A	Q	T	T	H	K	I	P	L	C	U	E	D	G
S	T	R	M	I	J	T	R	T	Q	C	Z	E	M
T	L	P	Y	K	T	G	A	H	K	K	E	Y	S
N	G	M	L	P	I	H	E	C	X	M	L	M	J
U	U	E	O	W	T	M	N	F	G	K	L	O	P
A	X	K	H	E	P	K	I	N	G	D	M	S	L
E	Q	U	G	K	I	G	N	C	X	P	R	T	K
U	P	D	M	I	S	S	W	A	T	S	O	N	L
G	U	Y	L	D	E	E	S	X	B	K	I	P	T
J	A	S	S	C	J	Y	L	E	W	W	A	K	B

Now match the characters' names to their descriptions.

1 This person is Huck's good friend. ....

2 This person sets Jim free before dying. ....

3 These two people get tarred and feathered. ....

4 This person is keeping Huck's money for him. ....

5 This person tells Huck his future with a magic ball. ....

6 Huck lives with this person before his father takes him away. ....

7 This person finds Jim asleep in the woods with a blanket over his head. ....

8 This person thinks Huck is Tom Sawyer. ....

Put the sentences below in the order in which they happen in the story.

- **A** The real Harvey and William Wilks came to the king's auction.
- **B** Huck and Jim saw a dead man in a houseboat.
- **C** Huck and Tom dug a hole into Jim's shed.
- **D** The king and the duke pretended to be Harvey and William Wilks.
- **E** Miss Watson always told Huck what to do.
- **F** The doctor treated Tom's bullet wound.
- **G** Jim told Huck the dead man they saw in the houseboat was his father.
- **H** The Widow Douglas and Judge Thatcher didn't let Huck's father have Huck's money.
- **I** Huck put the bag of money in Peter Wilks's coffin.
- **J** Huck's father took him away and locked him up in an old, empty house.
- **K** Tom told everyone who he and Huck really were.

1 ☐ 2 ☐ 3 ☐ 4 ☐ 5 ☐ 6 ☐ 7 ☐ 8 ☐ 9 ☐ 10 ☐ 11 ☐

EXIT TEST 2

1 COMPREHENSION

Answer these questions.

1 How did Huck know his father was in St Petersburg?

....

2 How did Huck escape from the cabin?

....

3 Where did Huck meet Jim?

....

4 What did Huck and Jim think of the king and the duke?

....

5 Why did the king give Mary Jane the $6,000?

....

6 Where did Huck hide the money? Why did he do it?

....

7 How did the people punish the king and the duke?

....

8 How are Jim and Huck both free at the end of the story?

....

2 CHARACTERS

Who did these things? Write the correct character next to each question.

1 Who looked after Huck and sent him to school every day?

....

2 Who asked someone to tell him his future?

....

3 Who didn't let someone have Huck's money?

....

4 Who took Huck away into the woods?

....

5 Who thought Huck was a ghost?

....

6 Who decided to pretend to be someone else?

....

7 Who pretended to be deaf?

....

8 Who gave the king and the duke the money back?

....

9 Who was sold for $40?

....

10 Who visited his aunt and uncle?

....

3 CROSSWORD

Complete the crossword.

Across

3 A religious ceremony you go to when someone dies.

4 A cover you use to keep you warm

5 Someone who cannot hear.

7 A title used for someone whose husband is dead.

Down

1 To make people believe something which is not true.

2 A person who is not free.

6 An event where objects are sold for the highest price.

The Adventures of Huckleberry Finn

KEY TO THE EXERCISES AND EXIT TESTS

KEY TO THE EXERCISES

About the Author

Page 9 – exercise 1

1 30 November 1835, Florida, Missouri
2 21 April 1910, Redding, Connecticut
3 Olivia Langdon
4 *The Celebrated Jumping Frog of Calaveras County and other Sketches*
5 Any of these: *Adventures of Huckleberry Finn, The Adventures of Tom Sawyer, Life on the Mississippi, The Prince and the Pauper, A Connecticut Yankee in King Arthur's Court.*

Page 12 – exercise 1

1 cave **2** woods **3** devil **4** cross **5** footprint

Page 12 – exercise 2

A 2 **B** 4 **C** 5 **D** 3 **E** 1

CHAPTER ONE

Page 18 – exercise 1

1 A **2** A **3** B **4** A **5** A **6** B **7** B **8** B **9** A **10** B

Page 18 – exercise 2

A 2 **B** 4 **C** 5 **D** 3 **E** 1 **F** 6.

TAPESCRIPT
(WD = Widow Douglas / H = Huck)
WD: Huck, come here, please. I must tell you about your jobs for today.
H: Yes, Mam. Here I am.
WD: Good. Now, as it is a lovely day, I would like you to do all the outside jobs first. You can start by hanging out the washing. Everything needs to be dry by tonight.
H: OK, I can do that. Then can I cut the grass? That's fun.
WD: Good idea. Herbie's very dirty and needs a wash. After you cut the grass, can you give him a wash at the back of the garden?
H: I can try, but you know what he's like. He won't stop moving and the soapy water goes everywhere.
WD: Ha ha. Yes, Huck, I know... But that animal loves you so much. He just wants to play.
H: OK. Then can I go and see Tom and the other boys?
WD: No, not then. There are still some jobs inside the house. I want

you to tidy your bedroom: it's a complete mess. Also remember to clean the floor and under the bed.
H: OK, I'll do that. Then, can I go out?
WD: Alright. You can go out. But one last thing. This morning I am making a pie for poor Mrs Richards. You know she is very ill at the moment. She lives near Tom, so you can pass by her house on your way.
H: So many things to do... I must start immediately.

Page 19 – exercise 3

$6,000 x 20 = $120,000

Page 20 – exercise 5

1 C **2** H **3** G **4** B **5** A **6** E **7** D **8** F

Page 20 – exercise 6

1 live **2** learn **3** find **4** hit **5** start
6 listen **7** hide

Page 20 – exercise 7

1 found **2** started **3** listened
4 hits **5** learned **6** hides

Page 21 – exercise 1

A PIG **B** CANOE
C HOLE **D** SAW
E BEARD **F** GUN
G AX **H** BLOOD

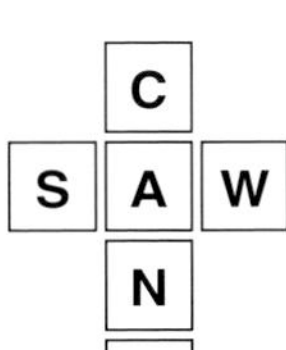

CHAPTER TWO

Page 26 – exercise 1

1 C **2** A **3** D **4** B **5** B **6** C **7** B **8** D

Page 27 – exercise 2

1 1, B **2** 3, D **3** 4, A **4** 2, E
5 5, C **6** 6, F

Page 28 – exercise 3

1 empty **2** new **3** careful **4** dirty
5 bad **6** clever **7** dead

Page 28 – exercise 1

1 canoe **2** steamboat **3** houseboat
A 3 **B** 2 **C** 1

CHAPTER THREE

Page 34 – exercise 1

A 5, GHOST
B 9, BODY
C 4, SLEEPING
D 1, RIVER
E 6, LISTENED
F 3, CATCH
G 8, FOLLOWED
H 2, STEAMBOAT
I 7, CAVE

Page 34 – exercise 2

1 having **2** ran **3** found **4** was
5 know **6** was **7** was sleeping
8 told **9** wanted **10** hope

Page 35 – exercise 3

1 C **2** D **3** A **4** B **5** A

Slavery in North America in the 1800s

Page 39 – exercise 1

1 A **2** B **3** B **4** B **5** A **6** B **7** A **8** B

Page 40 – exercise 1

1 A **2** B **3** B **4** A

CHAPTER **FOUR**

Page 45 – exercise 1

1 B **2** B **3** A **4** A **5** B **6** A

Page 45 – exercise 2

1 C **2** A **3** E **4** D **5** F

Page 46 – exercise 3

1 I **2** and **3** For **4** are **5** me **6** how **7** him **8** be **9** to **10** will

Page 46 – exercise 4

1 C **2** C **3** A **4** B **5** B **6** C

TAPESCRIPT

Well, how can I start? I suppose I can tell you about how I met the "king". It was a few years ago now. I wasn't working and times were difficult. One day this man arrived in the town and came to talk to me. I suppose I knew he was a bit of a fraud, but I wasn't sure. He had a really convincing way of seeming to be an honest man. I was very interested and I wanted to find out more about him. We talked about his life and his travels. He liked visiting many different places all over the country, but he really liked the South. For him life was easier in the South. The people in the North had stricter laws. I found out he was bored of traveling alone and was looking for someone to join him. He had quite a lot of money with him. I understood that I could also earn a lot of money. What choice did I have? There was no work for me and I didn't have any experience or any friends. I don't really like what I do, but I am good at it. We only take from people who have a lot of money: they don't need so much. This is the only way I know how to survive.

Page 47 – exercise 5

1 helping two slaves to escape
2 killing his wife
3 stealing an apple
4 stealing a lot of money

Page 47 – exercise 6

A 1 **B** 4 **C** 2 **D** 3

TAPESCRIPT

1 My name's John and I come from a very poor family. My mother just had another baby, so I now have eight brothers and sisters. We all live in one small room and we don't have much to eat. Sometimes I have to take some food, like an apple or an orange, from the market. Usually I'm really quick and I can run away before anyone sees me. But yesterday I hurt my foot and couldn't run. I was arrested and now I must wait for my punishment.
2 You can call me Doc, I suppose. I don't really have a home because I travel a lot. I often stay with rich families: they think I am a very honest man. So I stay with them for a while and then, when I have the opportunity, I take their money, jewels and other precious items. It's really easy, you just have to wait for the right moment. At the moment I am wanted in five different states. I must not get arrested because I think the punishment would be heavy.

3 I live in the North and things are very different. I first started thinking about the problems in the South a few years ago. My husband was traveling for business and he met some slaves. He then told me about their lives. I think it's absolutely terrible. That's why I do what I do. I must help them escape. I hang a lantern outside my house so any slave will know that the house is safe. Then I help them move onto the next place. Sometimes it is dangerous. I'm not worried about me, but I do feel that I need to stay out of trouble so I can help more runaway slaves.

4 I am a slave in a town near the Mississippi River. I live on a plantation and I work in the fields. Until recently I lived with my wife in a small cabin. My wife was very ill, but the master wouldn't let her stay in bed. She had to work and work. Things just got worse for her and she couldn't move. That was the moment when she asked me... I didn't want to, but she kept asking me. The master still wanted her to work and she was dying. So I helped her die. Now, I don't know what will happen to me. I can't read or write, so I don't know what is in the newspapers.

Page 48 – exercise 1

1 to count **2** servant **3** to smile
4 to hug **5** coffin **6** tears

Page 48 – exercise 2

1 servant **2** coffin **3** hugged
4 Tears **5** counted **6** smiled

CHAPTER FIVE

Page 54 – exercise 1

1 The king was Harvey, the duke was William, and Huck was their servant.
2 Because he spoke like an Englishman and they all wore new clothes.
3 Peter Wilks was the girls' uncle.
4 Because he thought it would be dangerous.
5 In the basement.
6 So everyone would be sure he and the duke really were Harvey and William Wilks.
7 She gave it back to the king.

Page 54 – exercise 2

1 C **2** C **3** D **4** D **5** C

Page 55 – exercise 3

A Mary Jane
B king, Huck, duke
C Mary Jane
D Huck
E king
F king, duke
G king, duke
H Mary Jane

1 B **2** F **3** G **4** A **5** D **6** C **7** E **8** H

Page 55 – exercise 4

A anybody **B** Somebody **C** somewhere
D any **E** somebody

Page 56 – exercise 1

1 graveyard
2 tattoo
3 arrow
4 lightning
5 mattress
6 auction

CHAPTER SIX

Page 62 – exercise 1

1 D **2** E **3** C **4** A **5** B **6** G **7** H **8** F

Page 62 – exercise 2

The men in your house are not your real uncles; they only want your money. Be careful.

Page 63 – exercise 1

1 tar and feather
2 cotton plantation
3 wagon
4 fence

Page 63 – exercise 2

A 2 **B** 4 **C** 3 **D** 1

CHAPTER **SEVEN**

Page 70 – exercise 1

1 A **2** C **3** B **4** C **5** C **6** B

Page 71 – exercise 3

1 C **2** B **3** B **4** A

Page 72 – exercise 1

1 pretended
2 nephews
3 else
4 climbed
5 over
6 believe
7 explained
8 hole

CHAPTER **EIGHT**

Page 80 – exercise 1

0 Huck and Tom made Aunt Sally believe they were her nephews.
1 Tom and Huck found Jim in the shed.
2 Huck and Tom dug a hole into the shed.
3 Tom hurt his leg when they ran away.
4 A doctor helped Tom
5 Jim found out he was a free man.
6 Huck found out his father was dead.
7 Everyone got their freedom.

Page 80 – exercise 2

1 Tom **2** Tom **3** Huck **4** Jim **5** Uncle Silas **6** The doctor **7** Tom **8** The doctor

Page 81 – exercise 3

1 A **2** C **3** D **4** D **5** C **6** D **7** C

Page 82 – exercise 5

1 slave **2** dug **3** freedom **4** lock

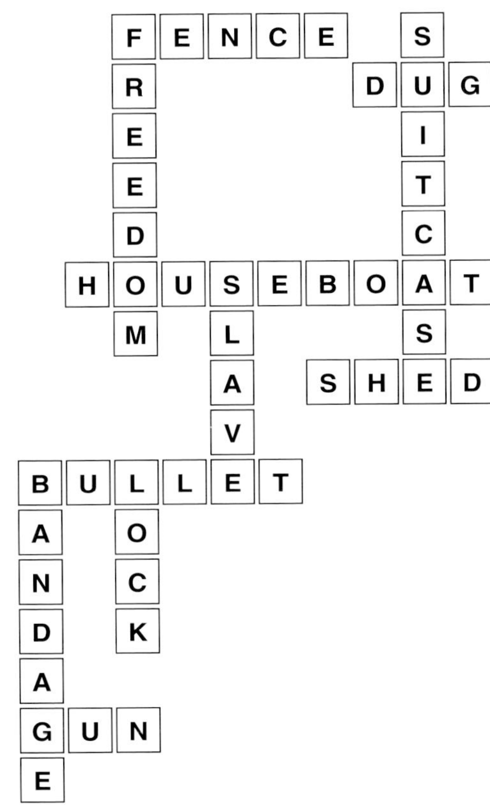

KEY TO EXIT TEST 1

Page 83 – exercise 1

1 Tom, **2** Miss Watson, **3** the king and the duke, **4** Judge Thatcher, **5** Jim, **6** the Widow Douglas, **7** Huck, **8** Aunt Sally

Page 84 – exercise 2

1. E, **2.** H, **3.** J, **4.** B, **5.** D, **6.** I, **7.** A, **8.** C, **9.** F, **10.** K, **11.** G

KEY TO EXIT TEST 2

Page 85 – exercise 1

1 He saw a footprint with a cross in it. He knew the print came from his father's shoes.
2 He made a hole in the wall with a saw, he killed a pig to make people think he was dead and he used a canoe to escape.
3 He met him in the woods.
4 They thought they were frauds.
5 Because he wanted her to think he was honest.
6 He hid it in the coffin because he didn't want the king and duke to have the money.
7 They tarred and feathered them.
8 Jim is free because Miss Watson freed him before she died and Huck is free because his father is dead.

Page 85 – exercise 2

1 Widow Douglas
2 Huck
3 Judge Thatcher
4 Huck's father
5 Jim
6 the king
7 the duke
8 Mary Jane
9 Jim
10 Tom

Page 86 – exercise 3

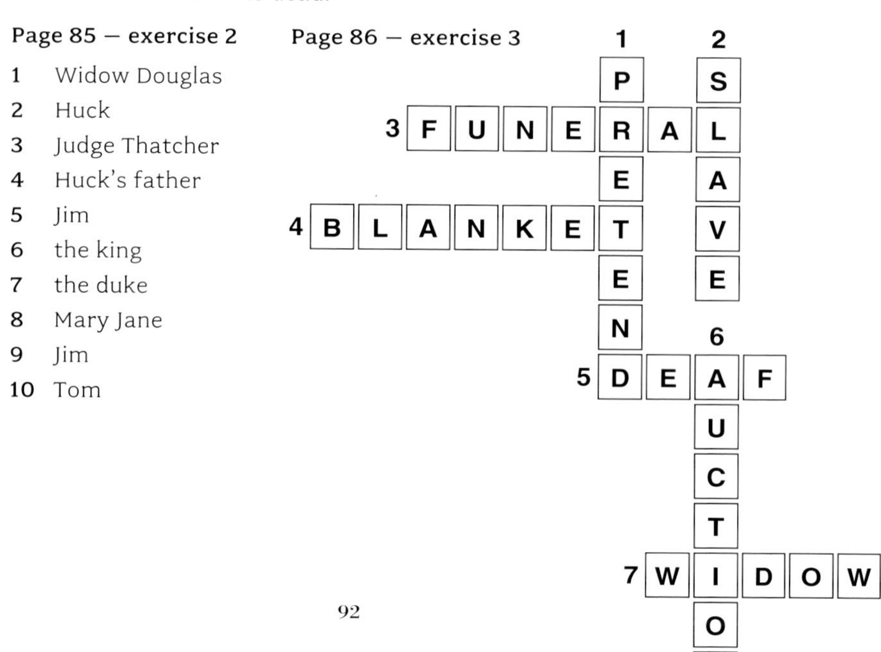

NOTES

NOTES

Black Cat English Readers

Level 1A
Peter Pan CD-ROM
Zorro!
American Folk Tales
The True Story of Pocahontas
Davy Crockett

Level 1B
Great Expectations
Rip Van Winkle and The Legend of Sleepy Hollow
The Happy Prince and The Selfish Giant CD-ROM
The American West
Halloween Horror

Level 1C
The Adventures of Tom Sawyer CD-ROM
The Adventures of Huckleberry Finn
The Wonderful Wizard of Oz CD-ROM
The Secret of the Stones
The Wind in the Willows

Level 1D
The Black Arrow
Around the World in Eighty Days CD-ROM
Little Women
Beauty and the Beast
Black Beauty

Level 2A
Oliver Twist CD-ROM
King Authur and his Knights
Oscar Wilde's Short Stories
Robin Hood
British and American Festivities

Level 2B
David Copperfield
Animal Tales
The Fisherman and his Soul
The Call of the Wild
Ghastly Ghosts!

Level 3 A
Alice's Adventures in Wonderland
The Jumping Frog
Hamlet
The Secret Garden CD-ROM
Great English Monarchs and their Times

Level 3B
True Adventure Stories

Level 4A
The £1,000,000 Bank Note
Jane Eyre
Sherlock Holmes Investigates
Gulliver's Travels
The Strange Case of Dr Jekyll and Mr Hyde

Level 4B
Romeo and Juliet CD-ROM
Treasure Island
The Phantom of the Opera
Classic Detective Stories
Alien at School

Level 5A
A Christmas Carol
The Tragedy of Dr Faustus
Washington Square
A Midsummer Night's Dream
American Horror

Level 5B
Much Ado about Nothing
The Canterbury Tales
Dracula
The Last of the Mohican
The Big Mistake and Other Stories

Level 5C
The Age of Innocence

Level 6A
Pride and Prejudice
Robinson Crusoe
A Tale of Two Cities
Frankenstein
The X-File: Squeeze

Level 6B
Emma
The Scarlet Letter
Tess of the d'Urbervilles
The Murders in the Rue Morgue and the Purloined Letter
The Problem of Cell 13

BLACK CAT ENGLISH CLUB

Membership Application Form

BLACK CAT ENGLISH CLUB is for those who love English reading and seek for better English to share and learn with fun together.

Benefits offered:
- *Membership Card*
- *Member badge, poster, bookmark*
- *Book discount coupon*
- *Black Cat English Reward Scheme*
- *English learning e-forum*
- *Surprise gift and more...*

Simply fill out the application form below and fax it back to 2565 1113.

Join Now! It's FREE exclusively for readers who have purchased *Black Cat English Readers* **!**

The book(or book set) that you have purchased: ____________________

English Name: ______________ (Surname) ____________________ (Given Name)

Chinese Name: ____________________

Address: ____________________

Tel: ____________________ Fax: ____________________

Email: ____________________

(Login password for e-forum will be sent to this email address.)

Sex: ❑ Male ❑ Female

Education Background: ❑ Primary 1-3 ❑ Primary 4-6 ❑ Junior Secondary Education (F1-3) ❑ Senior Secondary Education (F4-5) ❑ Matriculation ❑ College ❑ University or above

Age: ❑ 6 - 9 ❑ 10 - 12 ❑ 13 - 15 ❑ 16 - 18 ❑ 19 - 24 ❑ 25 - 34 ❑ 35 - 44 ❑ 45 - 54 ❑ 55 or above

Occupation: ❑ Student ❑ Teacher ❑ White Collar ❑ Blue Collar ❑ Professional ❑ Manager ❑ Business Owner ❑ Housewife ❑ Others (please specify: ______________)

As a member, what would you like **BLACK CAT ENGLISH CLUB** to offer:

❑ Member gathering/ party ❑ English class with native teacher ❑ English competition
❑ Newsletter ❑ Online sharing ❑ Book fair
❑ Book discount ❑ Others (please specify: ____________________)

Other suggestions to **BLACK CAT ENGLISH CLUB**:

____

Please sign here: ____________________

(Date: ____________________)